"You have to decide you want to be happy."

What if you fail? Locking yourself away in your studio is so safe; you don't have to put yourself to the test. What if you get to Paris and prove you're a great big failure? What if you go all that way and they don't want you anymore, just like Blake didn't?

Okay, I thought. They lay Paris in your lap and you have to think about it? Oh, just kill me now. Or ask your son what he thinks about this....

And Ben had two simple sentences for me:

"Are you crazy, Mom? Go for it."

Go for it.

I was finally going *far away*.

I was going to Paris.

Nancy Robards Thompson

Nancy Robards Thompson has reinvented herself numerous times. In the process, she's worked a myriad of jobs, including newspaper reporting; television show stand-in; production and casting extras for movies; and several mind-numbing jobs in the fashion industry and public relations. She earned a degree in journalism only to realize that reporting "just the facts" bored her silly. Much more content to report to her muse, Nancy has found Nirvana doing what she loves most— writing romance fiction full-time. Since hanging up her press pass, this two-time nominee for the Romance Writers of America's Golden Heart struck gold in July 2002 when she won the award. She lives in Orlando, Florida, with her husband, Michael, their daughter, and three cats, but that doesn't stop her from dreaming of a life as a bohemian writer in Paris.

What Happens in Paris

(STAYS IN PARIS?)

Nancy Robards Thompson

WHAT HAPPENS IN PARIS (STAYS IN PARIS?)

copyright © 2006 by Nancy Robards Thompson

isbn 0373230567

This edition published by arrangement with Harlequin Books S.A.

TheNextNovel.com

 HARLEQUIN®

PRINTED IN U.S.A.

Dear Reader,

I'm a firm believer in the old adage, "When one door closes a window opens." Because sometimes what seems to be a devastating end is actually a blessed beginning, a window of opportunity to a better life path.

That's exactly what happens to Annabelle Essex in my NEXT novel, *What Happens in Paris (Stays in Paris?)*. The end of her marriage opens the door for her to discover her authentic self and fulfill unrequited dreams. When life pushes her out of her comfort zone, she steps up to the challenge with grace and dignity (after an initial period of kicking, screaming and cursing fate). In the end, her courage is rewarded in ways she could never have imagined had she not faced her dark hour.

Life does move in mysterious ways. Sooner or later, change knocks at everyone's door. Sometimes we face the challenges willingly; often it's with a great deal of angst and trepidation. The next time you find yourself standing at life's crossroad, I wish you the courage to take a leap of faith that will land you on your best path.

Warmly,

Nancy Robards Thompson

This book is dedicated to Michael and that kiss we shared on the quay of the River Seine. Here's to many more. *Je t'aime*.

And to Jennifer, who patiently understands that the only way books get written is when Mommy spends long stretches of uninterrupted time at the computer. Jen, you are my sunshine. *Je t'aime*.

Acknowledgments

Thanks to my editor, Gail Chasan, Tara Gavin and all the wonderful people at Harlequin who make it possible for me to do what I love.

Thanks to my agent, Michelle Grajkowski, for everything!

Thanks to my critique partners, Teresa Brown, Elizabeth Grainger and Catherine Kean, who make the hard parts of writing fun. Special thanks to Elizabeth for double-checking my French.

I couldn't have written this book without valuable insight from attorney Adam Reiss. Thanks for the lowdown on laws pertaining to lewd and lascivious behavior, bailing oneself out of jail and filling me in on other—umm—interesting aspects of getting arrested; and special thanks to my good friend Carol Reiss, who did not bat an eye when I told her I needed to discuss lewd and lasciviousness with her husband. It's all in a day's work, right?

"*Grandmère*, marriage is sacred," says the girl.

The old lady quivers. "*Love* is sacred," she replies. "Often, marriage and love have no connection. You get married to found a family and you found a family to constitute society. Society cannot do without marriage. If society is a chain, then every family is a link in that chain. When one gets married, one is bound to respect a social code…but one may love twenty times because nature has made us that way inclined. You see, marriage is a law, and love is an instinct that moves us to the right or to the left."

—*Conseils d'une Grandmère*, Guy de Maupassant (1850–1893)

CHAPTER 1

My first clue should have been the infestation of gold-embossed, cream-linen envelopes from various law firms. Thirty-three of them I counted in our mailbox on that otherwise ordinary Friday evening. Each one addressed to my husband, Blake Essex.

My second hint should have been the way Blake swept them out of sight, nonchalantly shrugging them off when I asked about them.

"Who knows?" he said. "If I had the money they spend on postage for the worthless junk mail I get, I'd be a wealthy man."

That was enough for me. I mean, he was right. We did get an excessive amount of junk mail. Just never from attorneys. Still, it was Friday night and all I wanted was a gin and tonic—not a fight. I'd had enough stress at work that week. The wonderful world of marketing can take its toll.

I shoved all thoughts of the unopened lawyer letters to the back shelf in my mind—the place where I stored nagging doubts and discrepancies that didn't quite add up but couldn't be explained—and mixed us a drink.

We went on with our Friday-night ritual as we had for the past eighteen years, politely working together to get dinner, cleaning up afterward, watching a DVD, performing our bedtime routine, giving each other a peck on the lips, and falling asleep, back to back, on our separate sides of the big, king-size bed.

Standard MO for an old married couple.

That's what I used to tell myself.

But now that I think about it, the letters weren't my first clue. By the time they arrived, it was as if the universe was at its wits end and had resorted to slapping me up the side of the head and shouting, *Open your eyes, you blind idiot. Can't you see the truth?*

Even so, I didn't put two and two together until the next day when my sister, Rita, and I were on our way to Saint Petersburg to catch Le Cycle des Nymphéas— Monet's water lilies—exhibit at the Museum of Fine Arts.

Rita was driving and I was reading the newspaper, skimming each page diligently to make sure the competition didn't somehow get a leg up on the retirement company I do marketing and advertising for, scoring free press in the paper. I'd finished with the main section and moved on to the local and state when I spied mug shots of two men that gave me pause.

One man looked like Blake.

I did a double take and realized the name under the photo was *Essex*. The other was of a basketball coach at one of the high schools.

Every little inkling lurking in the murky shadows of my subconscious jumped to attention and my worst fears were confirmed—right there for all of central Florida to read in twelve-point type.

My husband had been arrested for lewd and lascivious behavior after being caught in a *sex act* with—*another man?*

The high-school basketball coach.

Thursday, they were caught in a secluded park in Seminole County. According to the paper, it's a place frequented by people—especially men—who are looking to exchange sexual favors. The coach had been arrested there before, but the school had no knowledge of his run-in with the law.

That's why the story was in the newspaper.

For everyone to read—

"Oh my God! Oh my God!" I was shrieking. I couldn't stop myself. "Rita, pull over. I'm going to be sick."

She swerved a little bit. "What's the matter?" She glanced at me, then back at the road as if she didn't know what to do.

"Just pull over. Hurry!"

She veered off onto the interstate's shoulder, and I tossed the paper in her lap as I stumbled from the car in the nick of time before upchucking my bagel.

The next thing I knew, Rita's hand was on my back and she was handing me a bottle of water.

"Here, rinse your mouth."

I took it without looking at her and did just that.

"Did you read it?" I asked.

"Enough to get the gist."

I turned to face her. Hot tears of anger and humiliation and disbelief brimmed and spilled. "Oh my God! What am I going to do? What am I going to say to him? To everyone who knows us? How could he let me find out like this?" I realized I was screaming because the words scalded my throat and I started choking.

Rita took my quaking arm and led me in the direction of the car. But I shook out of her grasp and stumbled back a few steps.

"How could he do this? I hate him! How could he do this?"

I landed hard on my rump in the sparse grass, in the midst of the sharp-edged rocks and sand, sobbing with my head in my hands. In the periphery of my mind I heard my sister urging me to get in the car, then I heard the crunch of tires pulling off the side of the road.

I looked up and saw a cop. Rita confirmed that, yes, I was okay. I'd just suffered a shock after receiving some bad news and needed some fresh air.

All I could think was, *Oh God, if the cop runs my name, he'll know I'm married to Blake. Then it dawned on me that this was how it would be for the rest of my life. Look, there's Annabelle Essex. She was married to Blake Essex, that guy caught having sex with another man.*

I put my head on my knees until I felt a shadow block out the sun. I looked up and the cop loomed over me.

"You okay, lady? You need me to call an ambulance or something?"

I wiped a sand-gritty hand over my face and shook my head. "I—I'm fine."

"Then get back in your car and move on. It's not safe to loiter on the side of the highway like this."

For a split second I contemplated that perhaps getting flattened by a large truck was preferable to getting in Rita's car and driving back to my ruined life. But then good sense rallied and I realized I'd rather be alive to torture Blake.

He'd have hell to pay for this.

I intended to collect in full.

Having your dirty laundry aired in the newspaper feels like standing in the middle of a busy street stark naked. No, it's more like standing in the middle of a busy intersection and not realizing the world is looking at you standing there stark naked until it's too late and—oops, the joke's on you.

Oh, look—I'm naked.

I'm standing here like a fool.

With that newspaper article, the whole of me was reduced to what was printed on page B-1 of the *Sentinel*'s Local and State section. Gee, all that and *my* name wasn't even mentioned.

It didn't have to be. Blake's mug shot and name spoke for both of us.

I'd been oblivious to the gawks Saturday morning as

I walked down the driveway to my sister's car to begin our drive to Saint Pete; blissfully unaware that the reason Joe Phillips next door stopped mowing his lawn and stared at me wasn't because he thought I looked hot in my new pink sweater that showed just a hint of décolletage. He didn't speak; didn't wave. He just stood and gaped at me across the stretch of Saint Augustine grass with a bewildered look on his face.

Ha! And I thought he was ogling my cleavage.

Later, when I realized the truth— Well, you can understand why coming to terms with Blake's betrayal would be even harder knowing I had to face people who'd read all about it in the newspaper.

Even before I knew, others were devouring the juicy details with perverse excitement because they actually *knew* the guy who got caught with his pants down in the park.

Oh, and his poor wife. Didn't she know her husband was gay? But they have a kid. Maybe it was one of "those kinds" of marriages...? What do they call it? A marriage of convenience?

How was I going to explain this to our son, Ben? He'd be wrecked.

Wait a minute. I didn't have to explain anything. I was not the guilty party, despite the guilt-by-association factor.

Or stupidity by association.

I had to stop blaming myself, thinking this wouldn't have happened if I'd been a better wife; a little thinner; more in touch with his needs....

More of a woman.

Or at least enough of a woman to keep my man from turning gay.

Rita and I drove to Saint Pete, but we never made it to the Monet exhibit. Good thing because I didn't want to forever associate Monet's water-lily paintings with Blake's coming out of the closet.

Instead of going to the museum, we walked on the beach. We must have walked for miles, me in my low-cut pink sweater that didn't seem so sexy anymore, and my sister with her sandals in her hand and her white pants rolled to the knee.

She let me talk.

"Ri, you weren't surprised when you heard about Blake, were you?"

She shrugged, pushed a wisp of short blond hair out of her eyes.

"Rita? Are you saying you knew all along?"

She opened her mouth to speak, but closed it on a sigh, and shrugged again. "Come on, Anna. He was just a little too..." She dragged out the word as if stalling for time.

Finally with a look of resignation she said, "He was a little too in touch with his feminine side. I mean, either that or you'd snagged every woman's dream man."

Snagged him? Was that what I did?

Blake and I never had a sweep-you-off-your-feet courtship. We met our senior year of college and dated for about two months before I got pregnant.

No snagging intended. I was as surprised as he was. I was prepared to raise the child on my own. He was the one who insisted he wanted to be a *family*.

Rita snapped her fingers. "Oh, I read something the other day where someone said something about a man who was 'just gay enough.'" Rita made air quotes with her fingers. "That's how I always thought of Blake."

I must have made a face because she grimaced. "Sorry. I probably shouldn't have said that."

Afterward, we mostly walked in silence.

Blake wasn't home when I walked into the dark house Saturday night. He slinked in rather sheepishly Sunday, late morning.

I sat in the living room trying—unsuccessfully—to distract myself with a biography on the artist Georgia O'Keeffe when he walked in.

He flinched when he saw me and shoved his hands in his pockets. Dark circles under his eyes hinted he hadn't slept well.

"I'm sorry," he murmured, looking stiff and pale and a little bewildered standing there in his pressed khakis, crisp kelly green polo and navy blue espadrilles that once seemed so Palm Beach, but now just looked…

I wondered where he stayed last night and how his clothing could look so fresh given the circumstances, but I refused to ask.

His gaze darted around the living room, looking everywhere but at me. He seemed so frazzled, like if I made a loud noise or erratic gesture he'd jump out of his skin.

It took a few beats to find my voice. "Why didn't you tell me, Blake? How could you let me find out like this?"

At least he had the decency to hang his head. "What was I supposed to say?"

"*Something.*" I set the book on the end table and pulled my knees to my chest. "For God's sake, anything would have been better than letting me read it in the newspaper."

He didn't reply, just raked his hand through his hair—he always messed with his hair when he was anxious—and stared at his espadrilles. I worried the fabric of my pink velour sweatpants.

"I didn't know it was going to be in the paper," he murmured so softly I could barely hear him.

I traced a zigzag in my pants' velvetlike texture and decided he was probably telling the truth.

The paper said his *partner in crime* was a high-school coach who'd been arrested twice for public indecency. The story admonished the county for its lax screening of teachers more than it focused on exposing the men who meet at Live Oak Park to exchange sexual favors.

Of course. Blake's name and mug shot made the paper because he made the fateful choice of having sex with the wrong man.

"Was this the first time, Blake, or have there been others?"

He took a deep breath and closed his eyes. "Do you really want me to answer that?"

"Never mind, you just did." Tears welled in the corners of my eyes.

"Would it make a difference if I said it was just a one-time mistake?"

I gritted my teeth before I answered.

"Do *you* want it to make a difference?"

I didn't hate myself for asking the question as much as I loathed the tiny spark of hope his words ignited. *Was it just a onetime mistake?* I held my breath, waiting for his answer.

All that followed was silence like cold water dousing an ember of hope.

Hope? Good God.

A bomb had detonated in our marriage leaving nothing but rubble; everything we'd built together blown to bits by his wanton act of selfishness. It nauseated me to think about it. More than that, it made me angry.

"We have to call Ben," I said. "Right now."

His gaze snapped to mine, a look of utter terror on his face.

I put my bare feet on the floor and pushed forward on the chair. "Blake, the story was in the paper, and it affects our son as much as you and me. People who know him have probably read it, and some wiseass is bound to call or e-mail him sooner or later and say, *Hey, I heard about your dad.* It's better he hears it from us first."

Blake closed his eyes and pinched the bridge of his nose. "It's Sunday morning. We won't catch him in."

I threw up my hands.

"Call his cell phone. He always carries it."

Blake shrugged, deflated. "Okay. Fine. Let's get it over with."

I turned off the reading lamp, which left the living room with its drawn curtains sad and dark. I tried to ignore the tightening knot in my stomach as I followed him into the kitchen.

"His cell phone is number one on speed dial."

Blake's shoulders rose and fell on a noisy shallow breath. He kept his back to me as he picked up the phone and dialed. Every muscle in my body tensed, making me second-guess myself. Were we doing this the right way? Panic screamed and threatened to put me in a headlock. Perhaps we shouldn't break the bad news over the phone.

Ben was in school at the University of Montana. It wasn't as if we could drop by and tell him in person. He'd come home for spring break just two weeks ago and wouldn't be home again until summer. What other choice did we have but to tell him over the phone?

"Hello, Ben? It's Dad. Did I wake you?... Oh, yes, I'm fine... She's fine, too. And you?"

He listened for a minute. I edged closer to see if I could hear what Ben was saying. I couldn't, but I noticed Blake's free hand shook as he raked it through his hair.

My God, he was really a wreck over this. I hadn't realized it until then.

I turned away and straightened my Eiffel Tower refrigerator magnet. Why was I feeling sorry for him? This was *his* fault. Facing the refrigerator, I folded my arms as if I could block out the emotions that were weakening me.

Then the stupidest thought barreled through my mind. What if, faced with dismantling his family, Blake realized the enormity of his mistake?

I mean he screwed up—*and how*—but should we have talked about it a little more before we told Ben?

I'd pushed Blake to make the call, and even though I truly had Ben's best interest at heart, part of me wanted to see Blake squirm to punish him.

He was squirming.

My God, the man was shaking.

Admitting a mistake of this magnitude to your son must be second only to confessing to God. Well, maybe it was tied for second because he seemed pretty wrecked that I knew—

"I'm glad to hear you're doing so well, son—" Blake's voice broke on the last word.

Oh…he was only human. If it was just a mistake, should he have to pay for it with his family?

Encroaching sympathy warred with the thought that Blake should have considered the cost before he dropped his pants.

I remembered a time when I was young. I tried to

steal a blouse from Casual Corner, but the store manager caught me before I could leave the shop. She scared
me to death, telling me that she could call the police
and have me arrested. She went on and on about how
this one stupid mistake could ruin my life.

In the end, she didn't call the police or my parents.
Instead, she made me promise never to steal again.

She let me go. She gave me a second chance rather
than ruining my life.

I learned from that mistake, and I'd like to think I
grew into a better person because of her understanding.

Maybe Blake had learned his lesson. Maybe we just
needed to talk about it, get counseling. It wouldn't be
easy, of course, but perhaps if we could surmount this,
it was a chance for our relationship to grow.

I reached out to touch him, to take the phone from
him so I could tell Ben we'd call him back later. But before my hand fell on Blake's shoulder, he said, "Ben, I'm
calling with bad news. Your mother and I are divorcing
because I'm gay."

After Blake left, the late-morning sun streamed in
through the kitchen window. It made my head hurt.

I slipped into the darkness of the living room, and lay
down on the cool leather couch, flinging my free arm
over my eyes.

Divorce.

He'd already made up his mind.

Ben took the news hard. I'd never heard such lan-

guage from him. Called his father a bastard. Said he
hated him and never wanted to see him again.

First, I was glad because I wanted Blake to hurt as
badly as I hurt. Then I felt guilty because Ben was hurting. My baby. It was hard enough for me to learn the
truth, but imagine finding out the person you'd looked
up to your entire life had lied to you.

I'd never been homophobic and had raised my son
to be tolerant of all people…. This was the ultimate test.
The logical side of me knew it was ridiculous to hate an
entire subpopulation based on the actions of one man.
Oh…but this was so personal. It hurt too bad to form
any conclusions.

While I sat at the café table in the kitchen, trying to
talk Ben down from the ledge, Blake disappeared upstairs.

He came back down after I'd hung up, and all he said
was, "Will you water the orchids, please?"

He had about twenty-five plants in a small greenhouse in the backyard. I knew they were valuable, but
I couldn't believe he was thinking about them in the
wake of what had just happened.

Selfish bastard.

"No. I won't." I loved flowers, but he fussed over
those stupid plants like an old maid. I didn't care if they
died.

"Fine. I'll come by and get them this week. When
would be a good time?"

"Should I get an AIDS test?"

NANCY ROBARDS THOMPSON   23

He squinted at my non sequitur. "Would it make you feel better?"

Anger sliced through me. "You are such a jackass. I don't want an AIDS test to make myself feel better. You had sex with a stranger—with a *man*. And my life could be in danger because of it."

AIDS was only one in a jumble of questions log-jammed in my mind, tangled up with the likes of how many sexual partners he'd had over the past eighteen years? Did he practice safe sex. Or did he think too lit-tle of me to do so? Even though we only had sex maybe once a year over the span of our marriage it only took one time—kind of like getting pregnant.

Only AIDS killed.

Turning onto my side on the couch in the dark liv-ing room, I drew my knees up in a fetal position and lis-tened to the sounds of the house that used to be our home—the tick of the grandfather clock, the phantom creaks and pops as the house settled; the refrigerator and air-conditioning that cycled on and off; and the full magnitude of how alone I was pressed down on me and unleashed the tears.

They came in torrents, in great heaving sobs that choked and nearly drowned me.

All the while, one single thought burned in my mind: How long would Blake have lived a double life had he not been involuntarily outted?

CHAPTER 2

The next day, I did what any self-respecting woman caught in the middle of an undeserved scandal would do—I called in sick to my marketing job at Heartfield Retirement Communities, then cut all the blooms off Blake's orchids.

Good harvest. About twenty stems with at least three flowers each. I gathered them into a bundle, tied them with a ribbon and made an exotic bouquet.

Flowers for me.

Originally, I intended to sit in the middle of the greenhouse and pluck off all the petals: He loves me… He loves me not, because he's gay and loves men… He loves men… He loves men not because he promised to love, honor and cherish me for all the days of my life….

That was just too maudlin.

The blooms were so beautiful, I arranged them in a crystal vase so I could enjoy them as I gorged on slightly stale *beignet*—that's French for doughnut.

I never realized orchids were such exquisite little works of art. They were always Blake's babies. I fingered a lush maroon petal that draped down past another cream petal shaped like a pouch the size of a chicken egg.

In the greenhouse, he'd labeled this one Showy Lady's Slipper Orchid. The name conjured images of cross-dressing, but I blinked the thought away and ate another doughnut.

I lifted the curious little pouch-petal with my finger. I'd never looked at an orchid up close like this, certainly not a stem cut free from the potted plants Blake sequestered in the greenhouse for optimum growing conditions (rather than optimum enjoyment).

I plucked Lady's Slipper from the vase, held it up and slowly twirled the stem in my fingers, getting a three-hundred-and-sixty-degree look at the flower.

Blake was going to be so pissed when he found his naked plants. He'd studied orchids like he was going for a master's degree, and coddled them, coaxing the temperamental things to blossom. All to end up in a vase on the kitchen table.

Oops. My bad.

Since we were getting a divorce it only seemed fair we shared them fifty-fifty. Florida was a community-property state. After eighteen years of contributing my fair share to our egalitarian marriage, I wanted my half.

He'd get the plant. I'd get the flower.

Fifty-fifty.

I'd downed seven of the twelve doughnuts by ten-thirty and was so disgusted with myself I decided I had to get out of the house before I died an unnatural death.

Death by *beignet*. Or murder by irate, flower-worshipping, estranged husband.

The thought made me shudder, or perhaps the thought of venturing out into the world?

I pushed the doughnut box out of my reach. It wasn't as if the paparazzi were camped on my doorstep. The sensible side of me knew the story of Blake's arrest had faded from the minds of most people in central Florida.

Old news.

But in my world of neighbors, colleagues and husband-and-wife acquaintances the story lived on. Suddenly *my world* seemed like the whole world; as if *everyone* knew.

I couldn't go to work.

I couldn't even walk out onto my driveway.

Good thing the car was in the garage.

After a few moments' contemplation, I decided to seek refuge with an old friend. A dear friend I'd neglected for a long, long time—my painting studio at the Orlando Center for the Arts.

I would go there and paint…orchids.

Because if I didn't get out of the house, I was afraid I might lock the doors and never find the strength to venture outside again.

I waited until I was sure most of the neighbors were gone before I grabbed the vase and drove to the studio.

Far better than staying home and eating until I couldn't fit through the door, or making myself crazy thinking about how I'd rearrange the furniture to make it appear as if nothing were missing once Blake took his fifty percent.

The only way to keep myself from dwelling on the ne'er-do-well was to focus on me. I'd neglected my interests—such as painting, and fresh flowers, and eating entire boxes of doughnuts—far too long.

I read in the Georgia O'Keeffe bio that she used to leave her husband, Alfred Stieglitz, for months on end to go paint in a place she called "Faraway."

It was only New Mexico, actually. I'm sure "Faraway" sounded much more romantic than "Alfred, honey, you're getting on my last nerve. I'm leaving now so I can refill my well. You'll have to get your own dinner, and pick up your own dry cleaning."

I know, I know, they probably didn't have dry cleaning back in those days and if they did, I'm sure a woman who had the gumption to go "Faraway" probably wouldn't have picked it up anyway.

My point being she took time to nurture herself, to foster her creative spirit. And Stieglitz was waiting for her when she decided to come home.

Paris would've been my "Faraway." Once upon a dream, I wanted to study art there, but life's obligations preempted those dreams. The big problem was that it was always so *far away*, and as a wife and mother, I had too much responsibility. Blake hated the French and had no desire to go to Paris. Not even for me.

* * *

After stops at Sam Flax for new art supplies (it had been so long since I'd purchased anything there, there was no chance anyone would recognize me) and Panera Bread for nourishment (frequent purchases there, but they didn't know I was married to Blake), I pulled into a parking space at the Orlando Center for the Arts. I sat in the car for a few minutes with the engine running and the air-conditioning blowing cold air on my face.

OCA sat at the crest of a hill sloping down to a beautiful lake. The compound was actually a series of old buildings united by lush gardens and courtyards. Fantasy architecture, I'd heard it called once, with Mayan/Aztec motifs gracing the aged concrete walls and bejeweled stepping-stones and fountains scattered liberally throughout the grounds. Red clay tile roofs graced buildings with worn cream stucco walls dating back to the early 1900s.

A magical place that always made me feel artsy and organic. As if anything were possible.

I picked up the maroon lady's slipper again and turned it around and around, trying to decide the angle I'd paint, but my heart felt so heavy I didn't know if I'd be able to drag myself out of the car so I could get to my paints.

Okay, Anna, you're starting over, who are you going to be now?

Good question.

I'd been daughter, sister, wife, mother. More successful at some roles than others.

What next?

In the rearview mirror I spied a smirking Mayan tribal mask etched into the garden wall behind my car.

"What are you looking at?" I murmured.

I could almost hear it answer, *He's gay. Is that what you want for yourself? Are you really willing to settle for a man who doesn't love you?*

My first thought was, *Yes, I just want my life back.* The scorned woman in me sounded a hearty, *Absolutely not.*

Feeling shaky, angry and vulnerable all at once, I stuck the orchid behind my ear, killed the engine and hauled myself and the vase of flowers out of the cool sanctuary of the car into the oppressive heat.

It was only March, for God's sake. It was never this hot in March.

In Florida, the relentless, lingering dog days of August were bad enough, but it was brutal punishment when the heat came early.

The weatherman said better days were on the way.

Yeah, promises, promises.

Until then, all the more reason to hole up in my studio with my big fat bag of comfort from Panera Bread—broccoli cheese soup, Caesar salad and a raspberry Danish—God knows I wasn't hungry, but I would be later. This way I wouldn't have to go out and get dinner.

I could stay there…indefinitely.

Or until I got hungry again.

Since I was still so full I'd probably never eat again. I was banking on a long stay.

I nudged the car door shut with my rump and adjusted my grip on the Panera sack, careful not to smash the Danish. The paper bag crinkled in my hands, and I had a brief second of panic when I realized pastry had been the sexiest thing going on in my life for a long time.

As quickly as the panic flashed, it dissipated. It was okay to turn to comfort food—

Comfort food and oil paints. The combination made an unlikely elixir, but what the hell?

The baked asphalt radiated heat like the basalt rocks they used in hot-stone massages. A brown lizard dashed across the pavement, heading for the grass, and I nearly tripped over myself to keep from stepping on it—or letting it scurry over my foot.

Logically, I knew they were harmless, but I had a lizard phobia. When I was a kid, one ran up my pant leg once at a picnic, and I did an embarrassing striptease trying to get it off me. I was traumatized. Ever since, they've made the hair on the back of my neck stand up, and I always end up nearly hurting myself trying to steer clear of them.

Classic case of once bitten, twice shy.

When I was in college, I studied phobias in a psychology class and learned they're usually traced back to an event that caused the fear, and when you're faced with similar circumstances, the fear and panic return.

My professor likened phobias to monsters we manufactured in our minds. Since there are no limits to our imagination, the only way we can dismantle the monsters is by facing them, by reaching out and touching them.

Beads of sweat broke free and pooled in my cleavage, teased by the hint of a breeze blowing in from the lake on the other side of the grounds.

There was no way in hell I was going to reach out and touch a lizard. In fact, the hot weather and the creepy-crawlies made me wonder why I lived here when there were so many other places I could go to avoid them—and Blake.

Ben was at college in Montana. I was free to go, if I wanted to. Just as the orchids cut free from the plant traveled to my studio where I could paint them.

The thought floored me. Did being free equal being unwanted? Cut free to wither and die just like the orchids?

I swiped at the moisture welling in my eyes— "Damn humidity"—and stepped into the grassy courtyard that hosted my studio. I tried to unlock the door, but the key stuck in the lock. I had to set down the bag and flowers so I could jiggle the knob.

It was mad at me for staying away for so long.

Fair-weather friend returning only after exhausting all other options.

After a little coaxing, the door opened with a squeak and I stepped into the shoebox of a room.

The shutters were drawn over the wall of windows and despite the darkness, the space was hot and dank. When I flipped on the light, it bounced off the white stucco walls.

A wooden easel stood bare in the corner below a cluster of cobwebs; a stack of forgotten blank canvases lined the wall; an empty coffee can for brush cleaner and a paint-splattered palette lay on the table, right where I'd left them the last time I was here—a good three months ago.

The first thing I needed to do was get some natural light into the room. I sidestepped a dead palmetto bug and screamed when I inadvertently dislodged a lizard carcass as I threw open the shutters. I couldn't even kick it into the corner.

The windows looked out into an adjacent courtyard. A large live oak shaded a blue mosaic fountain surrounded by an overgrowth of purple foxgloves, red, white and pink impatiens, hibiscus and azaleas.

It took me back to the day Blake brought me here the first time, when he leased the studio for me. Art was where we connected. When all else failed in our relationship—when we went months without touching—I'd return to his support of the creative me.

It was hard not to slip into doubt. Since he was not who he pretended to be, did that mean everything else he upheld was a lie, too?

How he said I was talented; that he loved me and wanted a family.

I mean, what was love? It wasn't quantifiable. You couldn't measure it by any means other than faith and feeling.

When we met he was a good man with a promising future as an architect. He treated me well, if not passionately.

There's more to life than passion. Passion was the flame that burned so furiously it burnt out and left you wanting.

I always believed a good marriage was born of the slow, steady rhythm of a man and woman, developed after passion flared and faltered.

Now I don't know what to believe.

We got married and four months later Ben was born.

I loved Blake. I wouldn't have married him if I thought he hadn't loved me.

I stood at my studio window staring at the courtyard, waiting for the pretty view to permeate me and work its magic the way it did that first day, but all I felt was empty. And hot.

Good God, it was sweltering in here.

I reached over and turned on the air-conditioning unit that stuck out of the top of the last set of windows like a boxy appendage. It chugged to life, shaking and rattling as if it would burn itself out before it cooled down the place.

Hmmph. Passion.

It took three trips from my car to the studio to schlepp in all of the supplies I'd picked up at Sam Flax— new paints and brushes, a large bottle of gesso and twenty more stretched canvases of varying sizes—I'd forgotten about the extras in the studio.

Finally, I shut the door on the outside world, determined to rediscover the joy of my studio and the painting process.

I started painting again after our son, Ben, began junior high school. I set up an easel on the screened-in back porch, but I couldn't leave my paintings out there since it was too damp. I used to talk about how great it would be to have a real space of my own; a spot where I could leave all my supplies and canvases—a real artist's studio.

The spot at OCA was a reward for sticking it out in a marketing job I detested. Since Blake had broken away from Hartman and Eagle, the architectural firm he'd been with for fifteen years, to start his own business, we relied on my company-funded benefits.

The studio was a compromise. Blake got to be his own boss. I got four walls to call my own. But I didn't have time for it, really. Working full-time, cooking and cleaning, raising a child and washing Blake's dirty underwear didn't leave much time or energy for creativity.

I'd bet over the five years I'd leased the studio, the cumulative amount of time I spent there barely averaged a once-a-month visit; that was more often than we had sex. Every once in a while Blake would get on my case about not using it and threaten to cancel the lease, which would force me to drag myself in there to create. So, coming here today, I decided that until I discovered my own style, I would paint flowers of all shapes and sizes, in the tradition of Georgia O'Keeffe; fragile Lady's Slipper orchids; big fat roses; vibrant sunflowers.

I set a large canvas on the easel and positioned the maroon orchid on a paper towel.

This would be therapeutic. I could mix the paint to any shade I desired; place it anywhere on the canvas I wanted. I could wash it on in thin, translucent wisps or glob it on in thick, heavy layers.

I set out the new tubes of oil paint I'd purchased, and one by one squeezed a dab of each on my old crusty palette.

If I wanted to paint roses blue, I could. If I wanted to render sunflowers purple—no problem. I might even paint this pretty orchid black to match my mood.

It was my choice.

Paint complied. It would stay true to whatever image I created. It wouldn't start out as one thing and transform itself into something totally foreign.

Unless I wanted it to.

I picked up the paintbrush, regarded the blank canvas and made a split-second decision not to paint the orchid. Nope. On my canvas, I would honor the traditional. I touched my brush to the glob of alizarin crimson.

Roses are red.

Violets are blue.

My husband is gay.

Shit.

Who knew?

The brush fell from my hand, *pinged* and clattered on the rough concrete floor. I pressed my shaking fingers to my temples.

Who knew?

Everyone in the world but me?

The small room started spinning, and I edged backward until my butt hit the wall. My knees gave way and I slid down until I half crouched, half sat.

I had no idea what came over me, but suddenly I knew exactly what to do to that canvas.

By the time Rita knocked on my studio door at seven o'clock that evening, I'd painted three canvases. Two florals and what you might call a *Picasso-inspired* portrait of Blake, though I've never been much of a Picasso fan. Rita likes him, but I've always thought of him as a creepy misogynist.

Appropriate inspiration for Blake's portrait.

I painted him with two heads (one male, one female), Medusa-like orchid blooms for hair and a spear driven through his chest. I'd used washes of blues and blacks with a spattering of bloodred applied with a palette knife for emphasis.

"This one's a little scary." My sister held up the canvas of Blake. "If he turns up dead, you'd better destroy this or they'll have all the evidence they need to hang you for the crime."

I shrugged, not in a jovial mood.

"What's Fred doing tonight?" I wiped excess paint off my brush with a paper towel, then walked to the sink to wash the residual from the bristles.

Rita and Fred had such a good marriage, after twenty-five years they were even starting to look like each other. Sometimes—especially after the hell I'd just been through—I wondered if my sister hadn't snagged the last decent man alive.

"He's at the all-night driving range, getting his golf fix. Where did those come from?" She pointed at the vase of orchid blossoms.

"From Blake's greenhouse."

Her blue eyes flew open wide. "Oh. My. God. If you leave right now, you might be able to outrun him. Let me rephrase what I said earlier. *He's* going to be the one hung for murder because he's going to kill you when he sees what you've done."

I smoothed the bristles back into shape and put the brushes in a jar to dry. "I know. I feel kind of bad about it. I didn't realize how pretty they were. Do you think he'll notice if I superglue them back on?"

Rita burst out laughing. "He's going to flip."

She walked over and picked up a painting of a huge sunflower I'd leaned against the wall. "This is nice.

Sort of Van Gogh–esque." She set it down and stepped back to view it, tilting her head from one side to the other.

"I wasn't really going for *nice* when I painted it."

My sister ignored me. "May I take it with me to show a client who lives in Bay Hill? The colors are perfect for her family room."

Rita was an interior designer and some of the houses she decorated cost more than I hoped to make in a lifetime.

"You know," she said, "we really should make some slides of your work. I could probably sell them for you. I don't know why I didn't think of this sooner. Are you coming here after work tomorrow?"

"I'm not working tomorrow." I picked up one of the brushes I'd just cleaned, dipped it in paint and drew a thick sienna line about a third of the way down the canvas.

"You're not?"

I shook my head. "I'm taking two weeks' vacation. I called human resources this afternoon and squared away my leave. They didn't even ask if I'd cleared it with my boss, Jackie."

I stole a glance at my sister, who'd crossed her thin arms over her tiny middle. She nodded.

"It's probably a good idea for you to take some time off. If you have the time, you should use it. What are you going to do? Do you want to go away somewhere?"

I shook my head and wiped my hands on a rag. "Nope. I'm going to paint."

Rita's eyes widened. "That's great. That's exactly what you should do."

What she didn't say was, *It will be good for you to pour all your anguish into something creative.*

"Plus, it will give us plenty of time to photograph your work. So, can I take the sunflower with me, Van Gogh?"

"Sure."

I watched my sister walk over and carefully pick up the painting and study it again.

Was it this kind of anguish that caused Van Gogh to cut off his ear?

What would Blake do if I sent him my bloodied ear all wrapped up nice and neat in a pretty little package? I could put an orchid on top of the box.

Nah. He wasn't worth it.

"Is the paint still wet?" Rita asked.

"Nope. That's the beauty of acrylics."

I tried not to get my hopes up, but I thought if I sold a few paintings, it would help offset the cost of the studio. I wouldn't be able to afford it when Blake and I divorced. Because I was sure once he saw how I'd sheared the blooms from his beloved orchids, he'd go for the jugular, saying I had to pay the rent on my studio because he couldn't afford it, knowing damn good and well I couldn't, either.

"I'll tell you what," Rita said. "Why don't you spend

the rest of the week painting, and I'll come over Saturday to shoot the fruits of your labor."

"Saturday? Don't you have plans with Fred?"

"Fred knows I'm on standby right now."

I rolled my eyes. Sweet of her, but I didn't want to become her charity case. "I'm fine, Rita. Really. In fact, I'm sure I can go to Target and purchase a roll of slide film and shoot them myself. Does Target sell slide film?"

"No, Target does not sell slide film. That shows what you know. Fred already has his heart set on golfing this weekend. So you're stuck with me."

Tuesday Blake came over for dinner. I hadn't seen him since we'd called Ben on Sunday, and I was a little nervous about the orchids massacre. But we needed to talk—to discuss money, who'd get what. All the things soon-to-be-divorced people talked about.

Nothing like a divorce to jump start the conversation. In fact, we had so much to talk about, I figured I could tell him I'd watered the plants and then distract him with conversation to keep him out of the greenhouse. It would work for now, and I'd make a point to be out of the house when he came to pick up the plants.

I wanted to meet in a restaurant. A nice, neutral, public place where things wouldn't get too intense (translate: far away from the orchids).

He insisted we meet at the house. Since he'd moved out, he wanted to look at everything and start making lists.

Lists?

Okay. Right. Lists.

That wasn't nearly as unsettling as when he said he hoped this was the first step to us becoming friends since we'd be forever connected by our son.

It just smacked of an HBO movie: *My Best Friend Is My Gay Ex-Husband*.

The absurdity really hit me as we sat in the dining room at our usual opposite ends of the long mahogany table. The dinnertime arrangement seemed natural when Ben was at home filling the empty space in the middle. We'd grown so accustomed to our places, when Ben left for college six months earlier, it never occurred to us to change.

To move closer.

Blake was his usual nontalkative self, but it was bizarre sitting there as we had countless times over the years, eating my homemade potato-leek soup, the ominous strains of Wagner filling the silence.

He looked so indifferent sitting there as if he belonged at my table. Sitting there in a clumsy, conversation-free standoff, I thought, *This is the man I married, the father of my child*, but I might as well have been staring at a stranger. Had he suffered at least a modicum of embarrassment or regret over the scandal? Had he lost clients? Was the thrill worth public humiliation and losing his family?

I was so nonplussed by his nonchalance that I meant to take a bite of soup, but instead the words "How long have you known you're gay?" rolled from my mouth like a piece of errant chewing gum.

"Annabelle." His tone was reprimanding, a blend of shock and annoyance, but he looked at me for the first time that evening, his soupspoon poised in midair.

The look on his face made me crazy.

"What? Does the word *gay* offend you? Do you prefer *homosexual* or another more veiled term? Tell me, Blake, because I'd like to know *something* before the rest of metro Orlando finds out."

His eyes flashed and he glared at me for the span of one deep sigh, before lowering his spoon. "I suppose I've known for quite some time."

The unflinching touché of words knocked the breath out of me. Reality slammed down between us like a thick sheet of ice. All I could do was stare at him through the surreal haze until he averted his gaze and resumed eating.

Hello? How could he eat at a time like this?

"If you've *known for quite some time*, why didn't you clue me in?"

He didn't answer me, but continued spooning soup into his expressionless face. I pushed away my bowl, and the creamy contents splashed over the rim. "All along I wrote it off that you were simply a man who was in touch with his feminine side. But you know, now that I think about it, it might as well have been written in big, bold script across the bedroom wall. How could I have not known?"

He shrugged and hunched over his bowl a little more, tuning me out. I had questions, and he was going to answer them. So I raised my voice.

"Living with you all these years, what did that make me, Blake? An idiot? Your beard? A fag hag?" Somewhere through the icy miasma of my anger I saw him set down his spoon.

He cleared his throat. "I thought we could discuss this like rational adults, but apparently we can't." He dabbed the corners of his mouth with his napkin. "I'll have my attorney contact yours. But in the meantime, I thought you should know so you can start making plans. We're going to have to sell the house or you'll have to buy me out."

"Talk to my attorney." *Don't have one yet.* "I don't want to move and I shouldn't have to buy you out, either. My standard of living should not change because your lifestyle did."

His chair didn't make a sound as he pushed away from the table and stood. He hesitated for a moment. I saw his throat work in a swallow as his long, manicured fingers worried a button on his shirt. I fully expected him to say something. Instead, he turned and walked out.

A dull ache spread through me as I watched the tall, slim man I'd tried so desperately to make love me disappear into the other room.

A few minutes later or maybe it was a few hours

later—who knows how long I sat there contemplating the ruins of our life—I heard the back door slam open. "What the hell happened to my orchids?"

CHAPTER 3

Saturday, as I painted the finishing touches on a still life of foxgloves, Rita appeared in the doorway of my studio clutching her camera.

It was still hot outside—so much for the weatherman's promise. The heady scent of gardenia wafted in, and I thought I heard the lake breeze whispering that relief from the stifling heat was just around the corner.

Be patient.

I was wrong. It wasn't the breeze or anything remotely so romantic. It was merely the air-conditioning cycling on, its cold blast merging with the muggy outside air.

Rita stepped inside and closed the door before the humidity flooded in and took over. "Ready to shoot?"

She set her Cannon on the counter and stood there with a funny look on her face.

"What?" I said, laying down my brush and wiping cadmium yellow off my hands with a rag. "I recognize that look. You're up to something."

She nodded. Smiled.

"Before we get started—" She pulled a split of champagne and two paper cups from her shoulder bag. "I have a surprise for you."

She set them on the counter, then handed me a plain white envelope.

"What's this?"

She grinned, nearly dancing. "Open it."

I did. Suddenly, I was staring at a check for seven hundred and fifty dollars—written to me?

"What's this for?"

"Your sunflower painting."

I squinted at her, confused.

"The sunflower painting," she repeated. "My client loved it. She bought it— Is seven-fifty enough? I guess I should have asked how much you wanted for it. But that seemed like a fair price. If it's not, I'll—"

"No, it's fine. It's fabulous. I can't believe you sold my painting."

With a look of pride on her face, she popped the cork and poured two glasses of bubbly.

She sold my painting.

She *sold* my painting. As I stared at the dollar amount, I couldn't fathom someone actually paying money for something I'd created.

Holding the check made me light-headed. This was enough for two months' studio rent with a little to spare for supplies.

Rita handed me a cup and raised hers. "A toast. To there being more where this came from."

Nice idea, but I was a realist. I painted for fun. I

painted for me. But for seven hundred and fifty dollars I could be commissioned.

Holding her cup, Rita walked to the middle of the room and turned in a slow circle, surveying my new work that lined the wall; in some places they were stacked four and six canvases deep, starting to overrun the small space.

She whistled. "You've been busy since the last time I was here, huh?"

I nodded. Thirty-three new pieces since her last visit.

"It's amazing how much I can get done when I don't sleep."

I set down my cup and shoved an empty plastic soup bowl—lunch from Panera again—into a sack and put it in the garbage as my sister walked over and flipped through a stack of paintings.

I watched her as she studied my work, and wondered what she was thinking. It suddenly seemed a little amateurish producing thirty-three paintings in the span of five days. Some artists agonized over a single painting for twice as long and here I was mass-producing them.

She paused to take in a brilliant pink camellia blossom, flipped past it and pulled out the close-up of the maroon orchid.

"Has Blake picked up his babies yet?"

I rolled my eyes. "He came by Thursday while I was here and whisked them away. The greenhouse is empty."

She nodded absently and gestured to the canvas. "I really like this. Reminds me of Georgia O'Keeffe."

My breath hitched. In O'Keeffe's biography she said, "Most people in the city rush around so, they have no time to look at a flower. I want them to see it whether they want to or not."

I read that she painted fragments of things because they made a statement better than the entire object. She created an equivalent for what she felt about something...never copying it form for form. I borrowed the same philosophy in the dark, almost morbid lines of the orchid close-up. No harm in borrowing a style until I found my own.

"Thanks, Ri, that's quite a compliment." I pulled out a stool and sat down.

"I'm serious, Anna. These are really good." She put the canvas back where she found it and picked up her purse again. "I have something else for you."

I poured a little more bubbly into my cup. "The champagne and check were plenty."

She nudged my hand with a slim packet of papers. "It's an application. Here, take it."

I did so, hesitantly, and set down the paper cup. "A job application? I have a job, Rita, and despite how I hate it, I'm not up for another major life change."

"It's not that kind of application. It's for an artist residency in Paris. Is this not perfect?"

"I'm sure it's perfect for someone, but I can't go."

She put her hands on her hips, and tapped the papers with her index finger's deep-red acrylic nail. "Anna, this is *Paris*."

She held it out again, and I took it.

Artist-In-Residence Fellowship—Call For
Applications.

The City of Paris, France, and the French Ministry of Foreign Affairs seek applications from foreign artists of any discipline who wish to participate in an artist-in-residence program. The winners will receive a monthly allowance and a three-month stay in a workshop/studio at the Delacroix International Exchange Centre, a former convent in the heart of Paris. At the end of the residency, one of the finalists will win a one-hundred-thousand-dollar purchase award given by the French government. The winner's artwork will become part of the permanent collection of the Museum of American Exchange in Paris, France.

By the time I reached the bottom of the first page, I knew there was no reason to keep reading. I shook my head and tried to give the papers back to her. She wouldn't take them.

"If you went to Paris, I could sell your paintings for you."

"You just sold one without me going."

"I know, but that was a lucky fit."

My heart sank. "A lucky fit. Gee, thanks."

"Come on, you know you're good, but it's the whole

French-mystique thing. My clients would just eat it up. The artist just got back from Paris."

"Oh, validation. That sucks. My going to Paris isn't going to change the way I paint. You know what Gertrude Stein said about a rose is a rose is a rose…."

"Right, but everyone finds Parisian roses a hell of a lot more appealing than the varieties we grow here. Come on, Anna, what's stopping you?"

Oh, let's see…my job. The fact that I was forty-one and broke and if I gave up that job, at my age I may not find another. And don't get me started on the huge ocean between the States and Europe and the foreign language I didn't speak beyond *bonjour* and *au revoir*. Even if I attempted to utter those words, I was sure some surly Frenchman would toss me off the side of the Eiffel Tower for butchering his language.

"I can't."

"Give me one good reason that doesn't have to do with your being afraid of something you've always wanted."

I closed my eyes and tried to put into words the litany of good reasons I'd just ticked off in my head, but all that came out was, "If I go I'll lose my studio space." Ridiculous—even I had to admit it. The absurdity hung in the air between us like a bad smell. Rita regarded me with a confused grin, as if she was waiting for the punch line of my bad joke.

"You'll forgo Paris to keep your rented studio?" She

looked around, and I could see her considering her words before she spoke.

"*Paris*, Anna. *And* you could sell your work to the French government for tons of money. What's not to love?"

When I didn't answer, she sighed. "They're choosing twelve artists. You have to apply. Cross the bridge about going once they offer you the residency."

I set the application on the table, feeling faintly sick.

"Just think about it," she said. "You don't have to decide now."

Working at Heartfield Retirement Communities was like living in a scene from George Orwell's *1984*. My boss, Jackie King—or the Jackal, as I called her—was always on red alert, watching and waiting for someone to screw up so she could sound the alarm and shine a great big spotlight. No wonder the day before I returned to my job as assistant director of marketing, I had a giant panic attack over what I'd face in the wake of Blake's arrest.

Exactly sixteen days had passed since the story appeared in the paper. I knew I couldn't hibernate indefinitely. The longer I put off plunging back into the real world, the harder it would be.

Cold hard reality dictated that since I was getting a divorce, I needed this job. Selling a painting had only lulled me into a false sense of security. Even if my attorney negotiated a decent settlement, I'd still need an income to support myself. Unfortunately, that meant that keeping my job had taken on new importance.

Talk about adding insult to injury.

Jackie King would almost smile if she knew how she had me under her thumb.

The Jackal rarely smiled.

Three of us made up the Heartfield Retirement Communities' marketing and advertising department: Jackie, the director of marketing, a real piece of work who had no life beyond her job; her administrative-ass, Lolly Rhone, who fancied she ran the organization; and me, the marketing misfit.

The Dynamic Duo. And me.

I'd been blackballed from their *club de deux* for a holy trinity of sins: my refusal to give my life to Heartfield Retirement Communities; my refusal to kiss Jackie's ass; and my blatant refusal to play their game.

I had nothing in common with Jackie, and she hated anyone who was different from her. She was a shop-at-WalMart-all-you-can-eat buffet-white-cake-bland kind of normal. Anyone too different, she mocked mercilessly (behind their backs, of course) for the term of her employment.

She cleansed her soul by going to church on Sundays and spending her vacations on mission trips to third-world countries where she built houses and shelters while her daughter stayed home with a sitter. Then she'd come back to work and treat anyone in her way like shit. But that was okay. She did church work.

She and Lolly were like two rotten peas in a pod. They traveled together, ate lunch together, socialized after hours. Jackie even baby-sat Lolly's kids. Yes, the boss baby-sat the administrative-ass's kids. In return, Lolly had her face so firmly buried in Jackie's behind she couldn't see their "closeness" bordered on incest.

We had our weekly department meetings—Jackie insisted the three of us have department meetings: one hour of hell consisting of a five-minute delegation of assignments for the week and fifty-five minutes of listening to Jackie's harangue about how her boss, Ezekiel Bergdorf, had screwed up the previous week and how she could have done so much better. She wanted his job as vice president of operations so badly she nearly foamed at the mouth. I was willing to bet that over time she would systematically destroy him to get what she wanted.

Therein lay the irony. Jackie's weekly rants left her wide open for me to cause her serious professional harm; it was as if she was playing career chicken, daring me to take her tirades to the brass. She knew I wouldn't do it.

I didn't rat on others (I'm sure in the catch-22 of her small mind she considered that a weakness) and I had no designs on her job.

Sad to admit, but I wasn't ambitious when it came to Heartfield Retirement Communities. I did my job and did it well, but come five o'clock, I was gone. Contrast that with Jackie-the-martyr whose life revolved around the company. She was divorced, had a nanny for her daughter and spent more time on the road than at home. She couldn't fathom why *everyone* didn't sell their soul to the company.

My marketing job started out as a temporary gig that stretched to twelve long years. In the beginning it was a part-time position that provided enough flexibility that I could work while Ben was in school—he was in second grade when I started—and leave the job behind when I went home. It allowed me to keep my foot in the workplace, but still take care of our son—

Who was I kidding? I used to feed myself that line of crap when I started feeling bad about not being able to be the room-mother for Ben's class or chaperon his field trips because Blake was adamant that I bring in my fair share of the livelihood. Heaven forbid that he be the sole supporter of his family.

Looking back, all I really wanted was to paint and be a mother to my baby (not necessarily in that order). My heart was never in marketing an overpriced retirement community. I suppose I should have left a long time ago rather than stay so long my boss regarded me as an inoperable tumor she was forced to live with because Heartfield never fired anyone—short of them murdering their boss.

No wonder Jackie had it in for me. She had no patience for a woman who preferred her child to climbing the corporate ladder.

Looking back, I should have done a lot of things differently. Now, all I could do was try not to look down as I crossed this rickety bridge over the canyon-of-major-life-changes. It was enough to make me contemplate curling up in a fetal position for the rest of my life. Instead, I walked in wearing my hair back in a tight chignon, the same as I had every weekday for the past twelve years. The place smelled of burnt coffee, carpet shampoo and office supplies, the same as it had every day for the past twelve years. I greeted our receptionist, Vicki, and started my approach to the break room to stash my salad in the fridge, the same as I had every day for the past twelve years.

"Oh! Annabelle."

I stopped and glanced back into an uncomfortable pause that lasted a few beats too long. But I reminded myself to hold my head up and look her straight in the eye.

"Yes?" I said.

"Um…welcome back."

"Thank you, Vicki."

Then by the grace of God her phone rang, and I beat a hasty retreat down the long hallway that contained a row of offices on the left and a liberal sprinkling of cubicles on the right. I made it unscathed, stashed my lunch and made myself a cup of tea (no break-room coffee, thank you, because it looked like dirty water and tasted worse).

Clutching my cup, I started to my desk, looking each person in the eye, greeting them. My personal life was *my* business, and I dared anyone to ask. But as I wound my way through the maze of cubicles, my co-workers honored my privacy.

Perhaps returning to work wasn't so bad. It reminded me of a little kid going to the doctor for a shot. The more she dwelled on it, the more it scared her, until she'd built it up to be something so monumentally frightening that even the thought nearly paralyzed her.

I'd turned going back to work into the mother of all shots. This wasn't going to be so bad after all.

Then I ran headlong into the Dynamic Duo.

There they were. Jackie was standing outside Lolly's cubicle, which, like it or not, I had to pass on the way to my office.

Jackie darted a quick glance at me, but kept on with her canned let's-pretend-we're-talking-about-something-so-important-we-haven't-noticed-Annabelle conversation. Good, maybe she'd let me pass without a passive-aggressive dig or contemptuous look. I was almost relieved, because I'd rehearsed this encounter in my mind, prepared several pointed comebacks I preferred not to use.

For instance, if one of them asked "How was your vacation?" I'd smile and say "Lovely, thanks." Or if I felt strong enough to volley, I could say "Why would you ask me that?" Then stare them down until they crawled into their respective holes, and then as I walked away say "I am not in the mood for your *crap*."

Good God, this was just like junior high school. Of course, since I was prepared, Jackie took another tactic.

As I walked past she said, "Lolly, hold my calls. Annabelle, good morning. Please come into my office."

Oh, shit. "Sure. Let me put away my briefcase and I'll be right there."

I was *not* prepared to deal with her one-on-one.

"Right. Take your time."

Take my time? She almost sounded... What was that vaguely familiar tone in her voice? Was she being... nice? Jackie King was a lot of things, but *nice* wasn't in her repertoire. She was too mean to be nice.

Oh God, maybe she *was* going to fire me.

Surely she wasn't *that* mean? She liked to pretend she had a conscience, and firing me now, when I really needed this lousy job, would be unconscionable.

She told me to take my time, so I did.

I shut my office door, placed my purse and briefcase on a shelf in the small closet. I closed the bifold door carefully so it wouldn't jump the track, adjusted the clip taming my long auburn curls, smoothed the back of my black skirt before I sat down at my desk and picked a piece of lint off my stocking before I started my computer.

The Windows logo had emblazoned the screen, and I had just lifted my mug to take a sip of tea when I spied Blake's face smirking at me from the five-by-seven gilded frame perched on the left corner of my desk. A vision of the mug shot that ran in the paper flashed in my mind. My heart ached as the hole in it tore open a little bit wider.

I pressed my hand to my chest for a few seconds before smacking the photo facedown and sweeping it—like a dead bug—off my desktop into a drawer.

Tears stung my eyes. I dabbed them away and gave myself a pep talk: I was not going to cry. He was not worth it. I closed my eyes for a good minute, until the burning subsided, then I took a deep breath, donned my emotional armor and prepared to march into battle.

"Annabelle, come in. Close the door. Sit."

Jackie's lips curved down, even when she smiled. She looked at me, radiating a forced creepy-warmth that made me think of the funeral director who helped me make arrangements for my mother's burial last year. An I-can-be-as-empathetic-as-you-want-while-you're-giving-me-your-money kind of look, but it wasn't money Jackie wanted.

Oh, no, no, no. It was details. I sensed it the minute I walked into her office.

She folded her hands on her desk, cocked her head to one side and looked at me. "I just wanted to make sure you were okay."

Liar. She didn't give a damn about me. She wanted the inside scoop—big fat play-by-play juicy details of Blake's arrest—and she was willing to make nice to get me to spill my guts.

"I'm fine."

"I wanted you to know I'm here for you."

Right. How about a pay raise and a transfer to another department? She'd never been there for me one day in the entire time I'd worked with her. And she'd be there for me now for as long as it took to get the goods and have a titillating oh-my-God-can-you-believe-that lunch with Lolly, because Jackie King was that kind of person.

It took me years to understand what this woman was made of—because there was a time in the beginning when I allowed myself to be taken in by her—and I'd rather ask Blake to move back and bring his lovers home than confide in the Jackal.

"Is there anything else?" My words were icy, yet I managed to curve my lips upward; not into a smile of gratitude, but one that closed this too-personal vein of conversation.

Her funeral-director smile faded to a nearly expressionless mask of comprehension. She unfolded her hands and crossed her arms.

"There is something else," she said as I started to stand. "I don't like the direction you're taking with the new marketing campaign."

She opened the file on top of her desk and pulled out my preliminary design for the new brochure—the design I hadn't shown to anyone yet. Where did she—

"Home is where the heart is… Heartfield Retirement Communities…?" She scrunched up her nose. "That's a little clichéd, don't you think? Come up with something else by this afternoon. We're way behind."

I glared at her in disbelief, trying to think of something to put her in her place, but as usual, my mind went blank with rage.

"Where did you get that?"

She wouldn't look me in the eye. "I peeked at your files while you were gone. After all, some of us had to work these past two weeks."

Some of us had to work? What the— Ohh, that martyr bitch. I was not out on a pleasure cruise and she knew it. She was just mad because I wouldn't talk to her about it. Even worse, she'd snooped through my office and taken one of my files.

"I need that back." I held out my hand and made a mental note to lock my desk from now on.

She closed the file and handed it to me, then started straightening the stacks of paper on her desk to avoid looking at me.

Coward.

Before I turned to leave, I stood there for a moment, towering over her, waiting to see how long it would take her to look at me. But she spun her chair around so that her back was to me and started typing on the computer perched on the credenza behind her desk.

She was a coward.

It dawned on me that the hardest parts of this crisis— telling Ben and going back to work—were over.

"You can leave now," she said without turning around.

Yes. Yes, I could. Perhaps it was time.

* * *

I smelled the scent of gardenias before I saw the movement in my peripheral vision. My gaze snapped from my easel to the doorway and there stood Rita in the threshold of my studio. I nearly jumped out of my skin.

Yanking off my MP3 earphones, I said, "For God's sake, you scared me to death."

She smiled and waved a stack of transparency sleeves at me. "Sorry about that. I knocked, but you didn't answer. Your car's out front so I figured you were here—wait till you see what I have." She sang the words as she shut the door and dangled a plastic sheet between two fingers. "I think you'll forgive me when you see these."

"The slides of my work?"

She nodded. "They look fabulous."

I set down my brush, tossed the MP3 player on the table and met her halfway. She pulled a small slide viewer from her bag and popped in the first image. "Here, take a look."

The boxy magnifier lay cool and light in my palm. As I pressed the button and the light engaged, the oddest sensation enveloped me that my future sat in my hand.

It was crazy—merely wishful thinking that I could make a living doing what I love, especially now that life was so messed up with Blake and I was ensconced in the new marketing campaign at work. All the ideas I came up with after Jackie vetoed "Home is where the heart is…" seemed trite and hackneyed.

I breathed in the heady scent of oil paint—I was experimenting with a new medium. It comingled with the gardenia essence that had marked my sister's entrance. I peered into the light box and saw the lavender foxgloves I'd painted last week. The delicate purple blossoms dangled from the stems like glorious pieces of amethyst standing out bold against the rich emerald background.

My breath hitched. I loved foxgloves and these looked good, if I did say so myself. There was a whole planter full of them across the courtyard from my studio. The slide reminded me of how soothing it was to lose myself in the painting process.

If nothing else, at least I had my art. Something to call my own, something constant in this world of madness.

Rita handed me another slide, and then another until we established a silent rhythm of viewing and changing. My discard pile grew. Her handoff pile waned. We sank into the comfortable silence that sisters weren't compelled to fill.

When I'd viewed the last slide, Rita said, "They look good, huh?"

"Yeah, they do. Thanks for photographing them, Ri."

She nodded, chewing her bottom lip as if she had something else to say.

"What?" I asked, putting the slides back into their sleeves.

"Don't kill me, okay?"

"Why would I do that? You're not going to tell me you've slept with Blake, too, are you?"

She scrunched up her nose. "Ew. No."

"Oh, I forgot, you're not his type. You don't have a penis."

My sister didn't laugh.

I held up the transparency of the foxgloves to the light and looked at it again, and when I looked over at her she shot me a weird sort-of smirk.

"You know it would be really good for you to get away from here. Go somewhere fresh where the word *penis* doesn't automatically evoke nightmares."

"What are you talking about?"

I nudged the last slide into place, skimmed the sleeve to the center of the table and turned my attention to Rita.

"You know I shot two sets of slides, right?"

"No, I didn't know that. Is it a problem?"

"Only if you hate me for sending them to Paris…with the artist-in-residency application."

I crossed my arms in front of me. "You did what?"

"I sent your work—"

"I heard you the first time. I just— Rita, I can't go to Paris. I told you that. That's why I didn't send them myself."

She pulled out a stool and perched on the edge of it. "I know you did. Your mind is kind of on automatic pilot."

I threw up my hands. "Well, I'm kind of preoccupied

trying to figure out how I'll take care of myself after I'm divorced. As of right now, that plan does not include moving to Paris for three months."

She looked disappointed and lowered her voice the way our mother used to when she tried to win us over to her way of thinking. "Why can't you see that would be the very best way for you to *take care of yourself*? A change of scenery, a change of career."

I hated this logical side of my sister. I walked over to my easel and picked up my brush. "Okay. Okay. Fine. I'm not going to fight with you over this. Thank you for thinking enough of my work…for thinking enough of me—"

The words burned the back of my throat, and made my eyes water. I swallowed hard.

"Thank you for doing that for me. But you know, you have to stop—"

I shook my head and stabbed my brush in the gob of cadmium yellow on my palette so hard the bristles flared.

"What were you going to say?"

Out of the corner of my eye I saw Rita stand.

"That I have to stop interfering with your cocoon-building? Well, I'm not going to, Anna."

I swiped a slash of yellow across the canvas. "This is not worth fighting over. Tell me where I can find a telephone number and I'll call and withdraw."

"Withdraw?" She laughed and stood behind me, but

I didn't turn around. "If you feel the need to withdraw, then you think you might win a spot."

I shrugged, and dipped my brush into the black paint. "I don't. I don't know what I think. Just stop."

"Why would you not go for this?"

A funnel of fear rose and whirled around my stomach, but I ignored it, focusing instead on how I should've been mad at my sister for putting me in this position; for going against my wishes and entering my work in that contest. And I would've been mad at her if I hadn't been so numb. But despite the numbness, deep inside in the very center of my soul, down in the tiny little speck of heart that hadn't frozen solid, I knew she was right. Only, there was a wide cavern between what I should do and what I was capable of doing just then.

"Well, Ri, I'll add *painting in Paris* to my to-do list right behind finding a decent divorce attorney and securing another place to live because Blake is barking about putting the house on the market."

She clucked her tongue and sighed. Loudly. As if she'd just learned I'd pierced my nipples and planned to shave my hair into a Mohawk.

"Look, it's easy to judge when your ass isn't on the line," I said over my shoulder.

"Yeah, I guess so. And I guess it's easy to use Blake as an excuse for not living your life. As big a bastard as he is, he's not the one keeping you from Paris. You're doing this to yourself."

I whirled to face her. "That is so unfair."

"I know it is. The entire scenario that's brought you to this juncture sucks. But Anna, what would really be unfair is if you used this crap as an excuse to curl up into a little ball and fade away."

I turned back to my canvas before the first tears broke free and meandered down my cheek. I wiped them away with my sleeve.

"You blame Blake for taking away your life. Don't give him your soul."

I heard Rita's sandals clicking on the concrete floor, walking away from me. I wanted to shout at her, *If I'd wanted to go to Paris I would have sent in the damn application myself*. Well, okay, I wanted to go to Paris. Someday. Just not right now.

Arrgh. Too much. Too much. Too much was coming at me too fast.

"I have a challenge for you." My sister's voice was softer. I glanced over to see her hitching her purse up on her shoulder.

"Don't withdraw. Just let the application ride. Toss it up to fate and see what happens. Okay?"

CHAPTER 4

After six weeks of having the bed to myself, I decided I liked sleeping alone. I woke up at six-thirty that particular morning smack-dab in the middle of the king-size bed. No one poked me in the back and told me to keep to my own side of the bed. No one elbowed me for inadvertently kicking him when I stretched out.

It was kind of nice, this newfound personal space. If I wanted to I could take my half out of the middle. It was a good thing, sleeping alone. I lay there and waited for reality to jolt my sleep-befuddled mind and expose the big dark hole that had taken up residence where my heart used to live.

I waited, but the familiar pain didn't stir.

A good sign.

Never mind that waking up was the easy part. Going to bed alone was still a challenge. After eighteen years of sleeping with the same person, I'd found comfort and reassurance in being able to reach out and touch Blake whenever I wanted—even though we rarely touched.

There was something in just knowing he was there, something comforting in the occasional brush of his foot against mine, no matter how unintentional; something in the rhythmic ebb and flow of his breathing; even something in his snoring, although until I discovered earplugs it used to drive me nuts.

I guess my newfound personal space—room to stretch—was one fringe benefit of living alone.

I spread my arms and legs to the four corners of the bed, just because I could, and moved them back and forth like a child making a snow angel. I reveled in the softness of the sheets under my body, and then lay spread-eagle for a moment, and listened to the quiet until the shrill ring of the telephone interrupted my calm.

"Annabelle, I didn't wake you, did I?"

Blake. My heart skipped a beat. "No, I'm up."

"Good. I wanted to catch you before you went to work."

His brisk tone hinted that I might not like what he had to say. But I waited, holding firmly to the old adage she who speaks first loses.

"Annabelle, are you there?"

"Yes."

"Listen, I've secured a Realtor, Jared Helmsley, to list the house for us."

"Excuse me?"

I sat up and swung my feet over the side of the bed.

Not quite a fighting stance, but at least I wasn't taking it lying down.

"I'd like to bring him by this afternoon to see the place so we can get it on the market as soon as possible."

"No."

"No?"

"No, Blake. I told you at least ten times already, I'm not ready to list the house." I'd just found an attorney to represent me and we hadn't gotten that far yet. "I'm not doing anything until I talk to my lawyer. So just cool your jets."

He heaved a sigh in my ear. A huffy, sissy sigh that irked me to the core. *Oh, be a man.*

He cleared his throat. "Annabelle, we're going to have to do something soon because my partner and I are starting our own business and we need the capital. I want my half."

Whoa! Wait a minute. Rewind. The implication propelled me to my feet.

"Your partner? Since when do you have a partner? You always worked better alone. That was the principal reason you broke off from the firm and started your own business."

He cleared his throat again. God, it sounded like a chain saw sputtering and dying in my ear, and it was getting on my nerves. I got to my feet and started downstairs to keep myself from snipping at him about the ugly noise. On the way down, I caught a glimpse of myself in the mirror on the stairs. Holding the phone with one hand, I tried to tame my wild curls, which sprang out in every direction and made me look like the Raisin Bran sun.

"Not that kind of partner. Jared Helmsley is my…
um…my partner."

I braced myself on the kitchen counter. It took a few
seconds before it sank in. "Oh my God, this Realtor is
your boyfriend? Well, you certainly work fast. Tell me
where you two met. No, wait—let me guess. Live Oak
Park, right? Aww, I love hearing about blossoming romance."

Not.

"Don't be crass, Annabelle."

Don't be a pansy, Blake.

"I'm retiring from architecture, and Jared and I are
starting an antiques business."

Antiques. How typical. My husband was a gay cliché.

So much for the small pleasures of sheet angels and
taking my half out of the middle of the bed. I needed a
good strong cup of joe after waking up to this. I picked
up my French-press coffeepot, measured water from the
refrigerator and poured it into the kettle to boil.

"Don't you think it's a risky move to cash it all in and
set up shop with a guy you just met?"

"I've known Jared a while."

"Like six weeks a while? Or longer a while?"

"Longer."

"How much longer, Blake?" I dumped some French-
roast beans into the grinder. I pressed the start button
and the machine hummed and chomped; the rich, ar-
omatic promise of a good cup of coffee lulled me into
hoping the day would get better.

He planned it this way, didn't he? He had to have some sort of Annabelle Happiness Radar that sounded an alarm when my misery dropped to a bearable level. Because just when I started to feel okay he'd fling another doozy. I turned around and picked up the glass pot, getting it ready for the fresh coffee.

"Jared and I have been together for three years."

I caught the answer just as the grinder stopped. The press pot slipped from my hands and shattered on the slate floor.

"What?"

He'd been in a relationship for three years?

"Did something break?" Blake's voice sounded miles away. But as far as I was concerned, if he were in China it wouldn't have been far enough.

Oh my God! Where was I when all this was going on? How could I have missed this? How could I have been so pathetically ignorant?

My free hand flew to my mouth, as much to stop the bile that was making its way up my esophagus as to contain my shock. My heart beat as if it were trying to break free from my chest.

As I moved around the glass shards, trying not to step on them with bare feet, I wished my heart would just break free and fall into the glass so that I could give it a decent burial. Like the coffeepot, it, too, was shattered beyond repair.

"Annabelle? Are you there?"

When he got arrested, not only was he cheating on

me, he was cheating on the one with whom he was cheating on me. Obviously Jared was a little more forgiving than I was.

I wanted to scream at Blake for being so callous, for making a mockery out of our marriage, for making me feel so utterly, disgustingly unlovable. For making me feel as if this were somehow my fault.

"Yeah, I'm here. But you know what? I have to get ready for work. No Realtors, Blake. Just—just go away."

I never got my coffee.

I didn't have time to tame my hair into my old reliable chignon and stop at Starbucks and get to work in time for the big unveiling of our new marketing campaign to the Heartfield brass. It was the trial presentation before we took our "new image" to the board of directors. I couldn't don my game face with wild hair.

So with or without coffee, life marched on.

For that matter, with or without Blake, with or without boyfriends and antiques businesses and whatever else Blake planned to spring on me around the next bend, I had to put it all aside and go to work.

Could life get any worse?

Oh, yes, it could.

Jackie had choreographed a boardroom extravaganza that rivaled Ringling Brothers. I'd spent the past two days assembling goodie bags with T-shirts, hats, key chains, pens and Post-it notes bearing the new slogan "Cutting-edge living for today's savvy senior" for Jackie to give to the Heartfield muckety-mucks after they finished telling her how brilliant she was for reinventing their image. She thought up the "cutting-edge" bit all by herself in a fit of martyrdom because "it reflects the new technology-minded older adult."

Because it provided the perfect opportunity for her to spend the better part of a week muttering about how she "had to do everything…" and how "the ineptitude in the office was killing her…." *Blah. Blah. Blah.*

I was surprised she trusted me to assist Lolly in handing out goodie bags and playing my role in the show: As she gave the preamble to the unveiling, Lolly and I were to put on sunglasses and walk up and stand on either side of the screen on to which Jackie would project her PowerPoint presentation. When she gave the cue, we were to whip off our jackets to reveal T-shirts with the new logo at the precise moment she flashed the new slogan on the big screen.

It was the cheesiest, most demeaning assignment she'd ever given me, but I guess Jackie got paid the big bucks to discern the gold in what we minions mistook for trash.

When I sat down at my desk, I hadn't even had a chance to turn on my computer, much less change into the T-shirt hanging in the closet or transport the goodie bags to the conference room before my phone rang. The extension on the LCD screen showed the conference-room extension.

"For God's sake, I'm coming. Chill out," I muttered to the phone before lifting the receiver.

"Hello?"

"Change of plans," Lolly hissed. "Bergdorf wants to meet with us before we unveil the new marketing campaign. Jackie and I are in the conference room. Forget the bags. Forget the shirt. Major change of tactic."

She slammed down the phone.

Did that mean I should meet *them* in the conference room or was this a Jackie and Lolly production?

I should be so lucky.

I decided not to leave it up to chance and checked to see if Jackie had a new assignment for me that Lolly forgot to deliver.

If worst came to worst and I wasn't invited, I could always seize the opportunity to make myself a cup of English Breakfast.

Perhaps Jackie had come to her senses overnight and realized what an ass she'd make of herself and us by having us flash the brass?

Better not get my hopes up until I found out what was going on. We still had a good hour before the scheduled meeting with the rest of them. Best not to celebrate prematurely.

When I walked into the conference room, Jackie was hunched over her laptop. She didn't even turn around when I opened the door. She just kept typing like a maniac.

Lolly was setting out Danish and doughnuts. The

coffee was brewing. God, it smelled wonderful, even for office coffee.

Despite the hold on the goodie bags and T-shirts, everything seemed to be forging ahead according to the original plan. Then I caught sight of Lolly's harried expression. She bustled around setting out cups and napkins wearing a grim look. Then Jackie turned around. She looked as if she'd been up all night.

"Could someone tell me what's going on?" I said.

Jackie and Lolly exchanged a glance, and Bergdorf walked in looking none too pleased.

Something was up.

I took a seat and folded my hands in my lap, eager to see what kind of mess Jackie had gotten herself into and better yet, how she was going to dig herself out.

"This better be good," he said. "Because based on what you showed me last night, the other campaign was a disaster. Maybe we should just reschedule the meeting and rethink this—"

"No!" Jackie's eyes flashed, but in an instant she composed herself. "Mr. Bergdorf, I was up all night putting this new angle together. I think you'll like it. The marketing department came up with the cutting-edge campaign…"

What? The marketing department did *not!*

"…and while I knew it was a complete departure from what we've done in the past. Well, let's just say, I now understand your concerns, and I think I've come up with a new campaign that will knock your socks off. Sit down and let me show you."

He glanced at his watch. "You have exactly two minutes."

"I only need one minute of your time." The usual superior self-assurance returned to Jackie's demeanor. But I thought I saw tiny beads of sweat glistening on her upper lip. As she turned toward her computer, she swiped her hand across her mouth and signaled Lolly to dim the lights.

Bergdorf pulled out a chair and sat down at the table, and Jackie started a spiel about how in recent years there'd been a return to family values. "Even though family values is a trendy buzzword—"

Bergdorf cut her off. "Can't you understand, our market share does not relate to trendy buzzwords?" He started to stand.

"Mr. Bergdorf, just hear me out, please. Actually, I think my new campaign will say it better than I can."

She pushed a button and the slogan "Home is where the heart is… Heartfield Retirement Communities" appeared on the screen.

"I hate her."

I said the words aloud as I steered the car onto Orange Avenue, but saying them only made me more furious.

She stole my slogan.

She stood right there and took credit for my— What did she call it? My *clichéd* slogan.

Of course Bergdorf loved it and fell all over himself congratulating her on the "brilliant comeback."

Jackie stood there soaking it up, a couple of crooked, yellow teeth flashing through her upside-down smile.

Shark.

Jackal.

Bitch.

She wouldn't even look at me.

No wonder she didn't mention my absence from the big unveiling, which I suppose went off without a hitch.

No way I was going to sit there and watch her take credit for something she'd loathed four weeks ago. So I went in my office and stayed there with the door shut all day. The only time I ventured out was to get my lunch.

She knew what she did because not once did she bother me. Not once did she try to explain.

"Annabelle, I was so frantic to prove to him I'm not a total loser that I inadvertently stole your idea. Come on, let's go tell Bergdorf that you're the author of the Home is where the heart is *slogan."*

I should have gone to the big meeting. I should have stood up and screamed "This is my idea and that conniving bitch is taking all the credit." Then I would have handed out all the goodie bags I'd wasted my time putting together so the CEO and the CFO and all the other acronyms in the room could see how much of the stockholders' money their talented little Jackal had wasted on all that useless collateral.

No, on second thought, I wouldn't have handed out the goodie bags. I would have dumped each one in the middle of the boardroom table and thrown all the notepads and pens and key chains up in the air like a bunch of trash confetti.

I would have stood in the middle of the table and pointed to the mess and said, "Hers. This is hers."

Then pointed to the big screen and said, "Mine."

"Hers. Mine."

Okay, so I wouldn't have really done it. But God, it would have felt good.

I was so sick of being crapped on.

I did my best, did what I was supposed to do, and for what? So my husband could leave me for another man and my boss could take cheap shots at me and then take credit for the very idea she'd belittled.

I was done.

I was over it.

If I could divorce my husband, I could—

I couldn't leave my job.

Not in a huff.

Once again, the reality hit me like a wall of water. I depended on this job I hated so much. Even if I left I needed the reference. I mean, after twelve years, I couldn't just walk away with nothing.

The only thing I could do was start searching for a new job. But where?

I was forty-one years old. Not exactly at the top of my profession. Who was going to hire me for the money I needed?

I needed…

I needed coffee, the whole day was so overwhelming. I drove to Starbucks and pulled into the drive-thru line. It was a long line. At five-fifteen you'd think everyone in the world would have had their fill of coffee for the day.

Okay, move aside, people. This is my first cup of the day and if I don't get it soon, I'm liable to take someone's head off.

The line moved at a snail's pace but finally, it was my turn to order.

"What'll you have?"

I'd planned on ordering my usual nonfat, grande cappuccino. But it was after five. I decided it would be prudent to order decaf unless I wanted to be up all night on a caffeine buzz walking the floor, brooding over what happened.

But something sweet sounded tempting, too.

A Valencia mocha?

A white-chocolate mocha? Ooooh, that sounded good.

But what about something cool since it was so warm outside? Yum—a mint-chocolate frappuccino. Mmm, it sounded like a dessert. But then again the—

"I haven't got all day, lady. Are you going to order or not?" The man's voice crackled through the drive-thru speaker. I blinked and waited for a laugh, a "No, seriously, take your time, I'm here to serve you when you're ready," qualifier—anything to prove the guy working the coffee line wasn't as rude as he sounded.

Stern silence followed his upbraiding.

He didn't have all day? What? Did he have better things to do? Was I keeping him from an important engagement? From a baristas' summit on world peace?

I could see it—coffee brewers of the world unite to further world peace.

Well, he could start practicing right away by changing his attitude. I didn't want to sit in this line shelling out four dollars and fifty cents for a cup of coffee any more, it seemed, than he wanted to take my order.

If I wanted coffee, I had no choice.

I deserved something to soothe my soul.

"Hello? I'm ready to order. Are you there?"

"Obviously. I have nothing better to do than wait for you."

Was this a joke? Hot irritation roiled through my veins. I wondered if I should warn him that I had a history of using coffeepots as weapons when pushed.

Instead, I took a deep breath, ordered a venti, nonfat, decaffeinated Valencia mocha and inched my car up to the drive-thru window.

Snippy Starbucks Man, who turned out to be a fairly decent-looking middle-aged guy despite the deep frown lines etched onto his forehead, greeted me with a frown and told me how much I owed. He thrust my large

Valencia mocha at me, then stuck his hand out for the money.

What is your problem?

I wondered if somehow I'd been transported to a world where all men hated women.

"Come on, come on, come on, already. Just pay me and move along." He spat the words, simultaneously snapping his fingers.

I think someone is a little caffeine cranky. He obviously had his coffee today.

I knew how to fix his wagon. I grabbed a handful of pennies from the car ashtray, matched his glare and proceeded to count the copper coins into his hand.

…ten…eleven…twelve…

He started muttering under his breath. The only words I caught were *lazy bitch* and *drive-thru.*

I stopped counting and looked up at his lined face. "Excuse me? Did you say something?"

His brows shot up. "I said it astounds me how lazy people are. They can't even brew themselves a cup of coffee much less drag their fat asses out of their cars to get it."

I opened my mouth to say something, but I was so appalled I couldn't form the appropriate words to do so. Finally, I resorted to the tried-and-true, "That was a very mean thing to say. Because we drag our fat asses here, you have a job. Why are you so angry?"

He rolled his eyes and something inside of me snapped.

"I'd like to talk to your manager."

He let loose a bitter laugh. "So would I, lady, but she's off today."

He turned over his hand and the twelve pennies fell to the pavement. Then he waved me through.

"I quit. So don't waste your time getting in a tizzy and writing a letter. Just take your coffee and go."

He stepped back. The drive-thru window slid closed like a final curtain, and I realized, with a heavy heart, I understood how a person could go through so much crap he became so bitter he lashed out at strangers.

The one thing Snippy Starbucks Man had over me was the courage to leave a place that made him miserable rather than sticking around waiting for people to throw hot coffee in his face.

No matter how much Blake put me through or how many times Jackie double-crossed me, I would not let them make me as bitter as Snippy Starbucks Man. Unless I intended to do something about it.

I took my twelve-cent venti, skinny, decaffeinated Valencia mocha and drove home, thinking that maybe later I'd go to the mall and get another press pot. Perhaps I'd get an espresso machine, too. My reward for not standing in the middle of the boardroom table throwing Jackie's useless collateral in the air like confetti.

The phone was ringing when I walked in the door.

I speculated it would be Rita and started formulating excuses for not seeing her tonight without hurting her feelings. She had been so good to me, but I just needed a little alone time.

All I wanted to do was savor my coffee while I read the newspaper that I didn't get to read this morning. I wanted to focus on stories about people all over the world who were worse off than I was and then sit back and count my blessings that even though life seemed pretty bleak, at least Ben was well, my car ran, I didn't have cancer and on and on until my list of how much worse life could be was so much longer than my current shit-list that my problems seemed to amount to nothing.

I contemplated letting the answering machine pick up, but decided that since I'd have to call my sister back it was better to beg off now.

"Hello?"

"*Allô?* May I speak to Annabelle Essex, please?"

The heavily accented voice on the other end of the line was most definitely not Rita—unless she'd suddenly become a Frenchman.

"This is she."

"Ahh, *oui*, this is Jacques Jauvert phoning from the Delacroix International Exchange Centre in Paris, France."

My heart skipped a beat.

"Congratulations, madame, I am calling to offer you a three-month artist residency at the Delacroix Centre."

* * *

After I hung up, I stood in the kitchen shaking. I vaguely remembered heavily accented mention of a plane ticket and paperwork to arrive within the week. He asked if I had a passport. Yes. Once I had a pipe dream that if I got mine, perhaps it would move Blake to get his and we would visit Paris together.

Key word: *pipe dream*. Blake had no use for the French and no intention of ever going to Paris.

I didn't tell Jacques Jauvert that story. I completely forgot to tell him I couldn't accept the residency.

Sure, it was nice to have my talent recognized.

Even better to have been given the nod by someone who knew something about art.

A French someone, no less.

All because of Rita. I didn't know whether to hug her or never speak to her again for getting me into this mess. I had to admit, it was a pretty flattering mess in which to find myself.

I picked up the phone and dialed her number, but hung up on the second ring. She'd be all over this. She'd come over and start packing for me.

I stood in the middle of the kitchen holding the cordless phone in my hand. The setting sun painted the canvas of sky framed by the window over the sink in hues of red, blue and gold. Inside, the room grew darker and shadows crept over the walls.

This was it. This was my ticket out of town. So why couldn't I—

The phone rang and my scream could have cracked the window. I almost dropped the receiver, but instead I managed to push the talk button and press the phone to my ear.

Maybe Jacques Jauvert was calling back. If so, I'd tell him thanks, but—

"Hello?"

"Anna?" Oh, no. It was Rita. "Did you just call?"

Damn. Caller ID.

"I did."

"Oh, we must have gotten disconnected."

"Something like that."

"What's up?"

I swallowed and tried to think of a last-ditch diversion. Finally I decided to tell her the news.

"You'll never believe what just happened."

"What? Are you okay?"

"I'm not sure. I just got a call from Paris."

"Paris? Who— Oh my God, Paris! The residency? Did you get it? Tell me you got it?"

"They offered it to me."

"Oh, wow! Oh, fabulous. When do we leave? I'm going with you. For a week, anyway. We'll go over early and do all the touristy stuff. My assistant, Tatia, knows this guy who rents his apartment by the week. I'll see if it's available."

She paused as if waiting for me to start singing the "Hallelujah Chorus."

"Rita, I don't see how I can go."

"I'll go with you and show you. I'll even come over and help you pack."

My palm clutching the receiver grew damp at the thought. Like I could just drop everything to jet off to Paris. If only it were that simple. Just pack a bag, jump on a plane and go.

"What about Ben?" I asked.

"What about him?"

"What will he do with his mother half a world away? He still comes home on school breaks and he's been calling home once a week to make sure I was doing okay since Blake moved out. We'd spend a fortune in overseas calls."

"He can come visit you once school's out. What college kid doesn't want to go to Europe?"

She was making too much sense.

"But what about the house? I've kind of been holding out on Blake, fighting him about putting it on the market."

"So throw him a bone. It won't kill you to let him have his way. It'll be more money for you to spend on calling Ben while you're in *Par-ree*."

Oh, for God's sake.

She was right. If I sold the house, I could pay off what little credit-card debt I had and bank the rest of the money. The mortgage and all the bills associated with it were the mainstay of my money worries. My car was paid for. Other than my studio, the house and half of Ben's tuition, I really didn't have any expenses.

Rita wasn't making this very easy by overcoming all my objections. What kind of sister was she? The worst part was she was making me feel like I *could* do this. Like all the planets were lining up to send me across the ocean.

"You should have been a salesperson," I said. "You're selling me on the idea, making it way too doable."

She laughed. "This is so doable you *have to* do it."

The sun dropped down below the horizon, leaving me standing in the dark.

"And what about my job?" I said. "What am I supposed to do in three months when the Parisian love affair ends and the government sends me packing back to the United States? What then, Rita? No job, dwindling savings, slightly better grasp of the French language— at least I hope I come away with that. Which reminds me, I don't even speak the language."

A bitter taste filled my mouth, but it wasn't caused by the language barrier. It was the memory of Jackie, the idea-stealing bitch, smiling her self-satisfied Jackal grin. "I won't even waste my breath on that one," Rita said. "You can move in with Fred and me when you get back."

"Oh, I'm sure he'd love that. There's a limit to in-law tolerance."

"I'm serious, Anna. If you give up Paris to keep that job you've hated for eleven-and-a-half of the twelve years you've held it, you deserve to be miserable."

Oh my God. She was right. "I deserved that."

"Perhaps, but you don't deserve to be miserable. That's what I've been trying to make you see. This is all I can do, Anna. You have to decide you want to be happy."

Ouch. I deserved that, too. Even though she didn't say it, there was something in her voice that said she'd propped me up as long as she could. It was time I started taking steps on my own.

Panic whirred inside my head, screaming things such as, *What if you fail? Locking yourself away in your studio is so safe; you don't have to put yourself to the test, put your "talent" on the line. What if you get to Paris and prove you're a great big failure? What if you go all that way and they don't want you anymore, just like Blake didn't?*

Snippy Starbucks Man's irritated visage superimposed itself over my mental picture of the Jackal baring her teeth. He frowned. *They lay Paris in your lap and you have to think about it? Oh, just kill me now.* He disappeared behind the sliding drive-thru window.

"Ri, I'm going to call Ben and talk to him about it. Let me call you back."

"You'd better."

Ben had two simple sentences for me:

"Are you crazy, Mom? Go for it."

Go for it.

I was finally going *Faraway.*

I was going to Paris.

* * *

The next three weeks were a whirlwind of packing, listing the house, putting the majority of my worldly possessions in storage, giving Rita temporary custody of the furniture our mother had given me, deciding what to take, what to trash, what to store and what to give away.

What does one pack for three months in Paris?

Starting over was like a psych evaluation if you really think about it: When it comes to "baggage" which do you choose:

A) Nothing. I'll start fresh when I get there.

B) Pack a single suitcase.

C) Take all your excess baggage with you.

I'd have to think long and hard about that one.

Blake's elation over my agreeing to list the house was short-lived due to my motivation.

"Annabelle, you can't just jet off to Paris."

"Yes, I can, and that's exactly what I'm going to do."

"Our divorce isn't final. Your taking off for three months will cause major problems with the proceedings."

"Well, that's not my problem. I guess you'll just have to wait, won't you? Your change of lifestyle has caused our family *major problems*. So I guess it's my turn, isn't it?

"I leave three weeks from today and I'm on a tight schedule to get everything done. When can you come over and take the furniture you want?"

"I thought you wanted to wait and go through the attorney?"

"As far as I'm concerned, you can have anything that didn't belong to my mother."

Rita called me before I left for work to tell me her friend's fashionable, sixth arrondissement, Saint-Germain-des-Prés apartment was available. The way everything was falling into place made it so much more satisfying to give Jackie notice.

When I walked in, her door was closed, so I told Lolly I needed to talk to Jackie right away.

"She's got meetings most of the day."

"I need one minute."

Lolly smirked. "I'll let her know."

I didn't trust her. I left my office door open so I could hear when Jackie came up for air.

It didn't take long. After about ten minutes of waiting, her door opened and her loud voice rang out over the office telling Bergdorf how she planned to implement the new marketing plan.

It still made my insides boil, but I was beginning to care a little less that she claimed credit.

She could have it.

I had Paris.

I walked up to her and Bergdorf in the hall and stood looking at them until the Jackal frowned at me. "Do you need something, Annabelle?"

"Yes, I need to meet with you this morning."

"Sorry, no can do. I'm booked all day. How about first thing tomorrow?"

"No, how about now? I quit."

CHAPTER 5

Three weeks later, our plane landed in Paris at seven-thirty in the morning. By the time we wound our way through the Plexiglas tubes of Charles de Gaulle airport, went through customs and claimed our bags, it was close to nine o'clock.

François, the driver Rita hired, stood in the airport atrium holding a sign that said, Essex and Roberts.

I was exhausted and overwhelmed but grateful Rita had the foresight to arrange for a car to pick us up. Nothing like traveling with a woman of the world to smooth out some of the bumps for a first-timer.

The first time she and Fred went to Paris they made the mistake of schlepping their luggage from the airport to the train to the metro, finally walking another seven blocks before they reached their hotel.

Never again, she insisted.

I could see why. It may have been nine in the morning here, but as I settled into the black leather seat of the sedan, my inner clock screamed, *Turn off the damn sun!* My body was still on eastern standard time, where the six-hour time difference translated to the middle of the night. I hadn't slept in more than twenty-four hours.

On the flight over, I dozed in a fitful half slumber. One time I dreamt I was chasing Blake, who kept running from me, just out of my reach, occasionally glancing back with a horrified expression on his face. I awoke shaking. The next time I drifted off, I dreamt I was lost in Paris, which had become a giant maze. I wandered in vain, searching, but not finding whatever—or whoever—it was I looked for.

I didn't bother to tell Rita about the dreams because they were so painfully self-explanatory. Besides, she seemed to be resting pretty well, snuggled up in her afghan with her eye mask firmly in place like a Do Not Disturb sign.

At one point her mouth gaped wide open and a line of drool trickled down her chin. I dabbed it away with a tissue.

My only solace was at least I didn't have my typical dream in which I realized I'd forgotten my passport as I tried to board the plane. Even if the new dreams were disagreeable, perhaps they evidenced I was breaking old patterns.

Safely on the ground, I was enthralled with my first glimpses of France, despite my grogginess. It wasn't quite what I'd expected. I guess I thought I'd step from the plane straight into the heart of Paris.

Au contraire.

Charles de Gaulle was about thirty kilometers outside of the city, a good forty-five-minute commute during the morning rush hour, down a highway that shot through an industrial area, gradually giving way to the suburbs, until Paris appeared, confident and proud, like an elegant lady. The buildings seemed to emerge from the River Seine like Botticelli's *Birth of Venus* rising out of the sea.

I waited for the scene to take my breath away, but lack of rest coupled with the excitement and adrenaline coursing through my veins blended to create a hyper-alert awareness of everything around me.

The light seemed brighter, the shadows deeper and more symphonic. The trees and grass looked a vivid, almost velvet green. I couldn't take it all in fast enough to satisfy my senses.

I was the worst kind of tourist, pointing and oohing and aahing over buildings and bridges, shops and flower stands. Everywhere I looked something new and exciting caught my eye. I saw François, who claimed not to speak a lick of English, stealing glances at me in the rearview mirror.

I didn't care.

"Look, Rita." I gasped and grabbed her arm, pointing to a great white domed building glowing high atop a hill. Set against the clear blue sky, it looked like a culinary confection or perhaps a sleeping giant overlooking the city. "What is that?"

"Sacré-Coeur basilica. It's up there in Montmartre, where all the artists and the windmills are."

We traveled a little farther and the City of Light whizzed by in a blur of tall, tin-roofed buildings, fountains and sculptures.

"Le Musée du Louvre." François gestured to a massive sand-colored building. It looked like faded gold in the morning light. I turned around in my seat to see it as we pulled onto a bridge and crossed from the right bank to the left.

"Le Pont Neuf," François said.

"He's telling us the name of this bridge is the Pont Neuf. It's the oldest bridge in the city," Rita said.

Finally, the driver stopped in front of a crêpe stand set into a storefront. It was part of a long row of businesses in this ancient-looking building that ran the length of the city block, in the fashionable Saint-Germain-des-Prés district.

Crêpes, the Parisian fast food.

He killed the engine. *"Voilà."*

My sister said something to him in broken French I could not understand. Then she turned to me. "This is it. The apartment's on the fourth floor."

I got out and looked up, counting up five sets of windows. The French count the ground floor as zero, and what we would consider the second floor they call the first floor.

So much to take in. So much to learn if I was going to live here for three months. The thought made my stomach dip. I glanced at the signs and advertisements, most of which only had a word or two I could actually read.

So much for four years of studying the language in college and the conversational French class I took in the weeks preceding the trip.

That was what it felt like to be illiterate.

A tall young woman knocked into me as she passed on the sidewalk. She turned and scowled.

"*Pardonnez-moi*," she said.

"I'm sorry."

She tossed her head and muttered, "*Américaine*."

Welcome to Paris.

I don't know why her disdain bothered me, but it did. All that was bright, shiny, new and hopeful about this strange place seemed remote.

In an instant my anticipation was gone, and so was the car and François. He pulled away, leaving Rita and me in the midst of the busy sidewalk with our bags at our feet and our vulnerability on our sleeves.

My vulnerability, I should say. My sister fit in like part of the ancient rue de l'Ancienne Comédie woodwork. Cars whizzed by and most everyone else moved with purpose, on their way to important places, I presumed, judging by the rush.

The overwhelming sensation of being alone in a crowd—alone in a foreign country—engulfed me, and I had a moment where I wanted to hit the rewind button and retrace my steps—back to the car, wind back the highway with the forty-five-minute journey to the airport, over the ocean back home again. Only, where I came from, there was no home.

Rita glanced at the piece of paper then back at the building.

It was actually a series of several buildings built one into the next so they formed a continuous row that stretched all the way down to the Boulevard Saint Germain owning the street; the four-, five- and six-story structures had magnificent windows in neat rows across the face. Some were adorned with shutters, others sported window boxes with red geraniums vivid against the white background; still others boasted stately grillwork that lent the humble casements the air of aristocratic balconies.

My God, this place was magnificent. And ancient. When Rita told me we were staying here I researched it and found out that most of the buildings on this famous street were built in the seventeenth century.

I tried to replace the cloaking wistfulness with a reverent awe for the history standing right in front of me, right under my feet. To think of all the wars and upheaval this place had lived through. In comparison, my problems were grains of sand on an antediluvian beach of change.

The thought humbled me.

I took a deep breath and turned a slow circle, trying to take it all in. Across the street I spied a Nicolas wine shop with a red awning that touted *Le spécialiste du vin depuis 1822*; a twenty-four-hour bread and croissants shop called Boulangerie de l'Ancienne Comédie; a hotel; a café with tables lining the sidewalk. Right next door was a…pizza shop? Okay, Parisian pizza. I suppose the French like pizza, too.

A sign hanging two doors down from where we stood gave me pause: Le Procope.

A chill ran through me.

Voilà—the world's first coffeehouse, where it was rumored Voltaire drank forty cups a day and Napoleon left his hat as security as he went scrounging for money to pay his bill. In addition to them, a virtual who's who of historical, literary, artistic and political figures, the likes of Balzac, Robespierre, Victor Hugo and even Benjamin Franklin, purportedly hung out there in their respective times over the past four hundred years.

It was too romantic, all that history.

I took another deep breath and let it all sink in.

I was in *Paris*.

Oh my God. I was *really* in Paris.

I waited for the rapture I'd always known I'd feel once I got here to unfurl inside me. But nothing happened. Just traces of the lingering wistfulness I'd felt since I'd disembarked.

Must be jet lag.

"I'm guessing this is the way in?" Rita, still worrying the folder with her notes, gestured to an unobtrusive brown door with a gold number six above it. The entrance faded into the shadows, overwhelmed by the red-canopied crêpe stand that stood next door. Funny,

I noticed the wine shop and the pizzeria, but number six rue de l'Ancienne Comédie slipped by until Rita pointed it out. Perhaps my oblivion to subtle detail had caused me to miss the telltale signs of Blake's secret life. Once my eyes were opened, they were there, right in front of my face, just like this plain brown door.

My stomach clenched; my heart weighed heavy and full, like all the pain would spill out of me onto the street.

"Must be it."

Well, I would just have to be more observant while I was in Paris. Here, I would learn to *really see* the details around me instead of wandering absently from place to place looking but not really seeing.

As we grabbed our bags and approached the building, I tried to see past the obvious to the sound of the morning traffic; to the way the face of the building lay in shadow as the sun crouched in the eastern sky. I inhaled the interesting mélange of aromas: savory crêpes, rich coffee, cigarette smoke and—car exhaust.

Not very romantic.

But it was real.

I guess one didn't step outside and think, *Lovely smell of traffic fumes this morning.* Okay, maybe that was taking detail a little too far. But how about the small group of guys who looked to be in their mid to late twenties loitering around the *crêperie?* Five of them, I counted, all talking at once, two sitting, three standing, the Frenchness of them claiming tangible space.

They seemed to be the only people in all of Paris, other than Rita and me, who were standing still. They weren't eating, didn't appear to be working. While they didn't look like a gang of hoodlums—this was Saint-Germain-des-Prés after all, it wasn't a ghetto—I wondered why they'd gathered there at this hour.

Perhaps I was distracted by the melodious combination of deep, accented man-voices; perhaps I was tired from the trip and intoxicated by all the different sights, sounds, smells and emotions, but I stared a little too long, until I saw one of the men staring back at me.

I looked away and tucked a flyaway, auburn curl that had escaped my chignon behind my ear as Rita tried for the third time to enter the correct door code.

The young guy who'd caught me gawking unfolded himself from a chair, did a smooth side step past his buddies, punched in the code for her and held open the door.

Oh, good, the entire neighborhood knew the code. That was comforting.

"*Merci beaucoup, monsieur,*" Rita sang, managing to sound confident and even a tad flirty as she hoisted her bag into the dimly lit vestibule.

The young man was tall and rail thin with short, light brown hair. He nodded and swept his hand, inviting me to enter. As his friends murmured in French and laughed in the background, the guy's gaze didn't waver from mine.

I felt so painfully American, it couldn't have been

more apparent if I had a big sign above my head with neon arrows pointing down at me. I managed to stammer, "*Merci.*"

He smiled again. "*Avec plaisir.*"

The words rolled off his tongue and a shiver skittered through my body. I'd always been a sucker for a man with an accent. Especially a French accent.

He quirked a brow, and I realized he probably wasn't much older than Ben. Perhaps six or eight years. I blinked to free myself from his lingering gaze and joined Rita who stood by a broom-closet-size lift.

The entrance hall smelled musty and old, the ancient odor merging with the men's cigarettes and the *crêperie's* kitchen smells.

"There's no way we'll both fit in here with all our luggage," she said. "We'll have to go up one at a time—or one of us could use the stairs."

She pushed the elevator call button. "The owner is supposed to be waiting for us in the apartment. Why don't I go up first and talk to him."

Fine with me. Her grasp of the language was far better than mine. The lift bell announced its arrival.

"Do you want to leave your suitcase here with me?"

Rita stepped through the doors and wheeled her obscenely small bag in next to her. "No, mine will fit." She motioned to my three suitcases. "But you might have to haul the green monster and family up five flights of steps. I don't know how you're going to fit it all in here."

The elevator door barely cleared her nose as it slid

shut. I took off my trench coat and protectively re-garded the "green monster," as Rita so fondly deemed my oversize floral suitcase.

"You could pack a family of four and their belongings in that thing," Rita had said yesterday as she watched her husband, Fred, nearly give himself a hernia hoist-ing my bag into the trunk before we took off for the air-port.

"Since I'm staying so long I have a valid excuse for overpacking. Be quiet and let me enjoy the moment."

"Touché," she'd replied.

With that justification smugly in mind, I gathered my luggage, scooting my other bags closer to the green monster and arranging them in ascending order of height. Since Rita had only packed one bag, I took the opportunity to bring a total of three: my two permitted bags and a third, which Rita checked for me.

Why not? Only an idiot wouldn't take maximum ad-vantage of the baggage rule. But now that I was here, I did wonder how in heck I'd get the excess baggage up-stairs.

"*Madame*, you are arriving in Paris this morning?"

The deep voice startled me. I turned and saw the guy who'd opened the door for us lingering in the thresh-old. Seeing him there made me stand a little straighter and finger the pearls hanging down on my cream cash-mere sweater. "*Oui.*" I don't know why I answered him in French because it only invited dialogue in his language—a language I didn't speak well enough to carry on a conversation.

"*Vous restez ici combien de temps?*" he said.

I gave him my best blank stare and he answered, "*Vous comprenez?*"

I understood his question well enough to know he'd asked if I understood what he said. It took a moment, but I recalled the appropriate answer.

"*Non, je ne comprends pas. Je suis Américaine.*"

"You speak a little French?" It was hard to explain the expression on his face—not a smile, but not quite a frown—as his gaze raked over my body.

"Just enough to get into trouble."

His gaze snapped back to mine and he arched a brow. I didn't mean to say the words aloud, and I bit my bottom lip to keep anything else from inadvertently slipping out.

A smirk teased up the left side of his mouth. "You like trouble, no?"

I suppose a more vulnerable woman might have been uncomfortable finding herself alone with him in the dim, dank entryway. But his words weren't threatening. *Au contraire.* How could they be, floating out there on such a flirtatious note?

The faint echo of the lift bell reverberated, announcing Rita's arrival five floors up. I glanced at the staircase and tightened my grip on the green monster.

"My name is Étienne. Are you married?" He stood much too close to me and offered his hand. Still gripping the handle of my suitcase, I put my right hand in his.

"*Je m'appelle* Annabelle." Reflexively, my thumb rubbed the bare space where my wedding ring used to be. Was I married? Good question. Technically, yes. Emotionally—

"No. I'm not married."

"*Bienvenu*, Annabelle." He pulled my hand to his lips, glancing up at me as he brushed an air kiss over my knuckles. He was cute. Long black lashes fringing caramel-colored eyes. But my God, he was a baby. How would I feel if some middle-aged soon-to-be-divorcée was picking up Ben?

"You are very beautiful," he said.

Oh, my…and quite charming for a boy half my age. Okay, perhaps not *quite* half my age, but close enough.

I suppose a more vulnerable woman might have been tempted to believe he actually *was* flirting with her. And technically, I guess he was—he was French after all.

According to everything I'd read, flirtation was France's second national language. But I was old enough and wise enough to step back and assess the situation: opportunistic, flirty French boy hangs out at the entrance of building containing short-term rentals. He spies two middle-aged—obviously American—women arriving alone in a foreign country…

It smacked of *Shirley Valentine*. You know, that movie in which Shirley, a slightly long-in-the-tooth housewife, gets fed up with her mundane life and takes herself on vacation to Greece? A handsome local sweeps in and seduces her. Poor unsuspecting Shirley realizes too late that her oh-so-romantic Casanova is actually a well-rehearsed cad who uses the same tired lines on the steady stream of middle-aged malcontents who flock to the island looking for love in all the wrong places.

Well, Flirty French Boy, I am not Shirley Valentine.

Flirty French Boy offered to haul the green monster up the spiral staircase after my unsuccessful attempt to cram everything and myself into the lift. With his offer, visions of Shirley V. evaporated and paranoia set in: horror visions of Flirty French Boy tucking me safely inside the coffin-size lift and disappearing into the streets with my worldly possessions.

"Thank you for offering, but I can manage."

I lifted the smallest bag onto the green monster. I could lug one in each hand. If I went slowly, it would work.

Looking up the stairs to the first landing made me wish I'd told Rita I'd send my bags up after her. She could have taken them off the elevator.

Oh, well. Schlepping was better than standing there doing nothing.

As I mounted the third step and pulled the bags up behind me, the small one slid off the larger one.

Étienne caught the handle and jerked it upright in

one motion. "Let me help you. I will not run away with your cases, if that is what worries you."

Well…don't be so pushy.

My cheeks warmed—from frustration or embarrassment? Perhaps both. I read once that some rapists ingratiate themselves to victims before striking. They offered help or some other random act of kindness and made the victim feel like an ingrate for refusing.

He was already ahead of me and halfway up to the first landing with two of my bags when I said, "You know, my sister is right upstairs. She'll be out to help me in just a minute. You really don't have to do this."

As we bumped and scraped the luggage up the steps, I lagged behind him at a safe distance, berating myself for bringing all this crap.

By the time I reached the third landing, I heard Rita's voice in muffled conversation.

"Fifth floor?" Étienne called over his shoulder from the fourth floor.

"That's right." I huffed out the words between steps. This was the secret to how Frenchwomen stayed so thin—through these sneaky mini workouts. By making the elevators impossibly small, they automatically weeded out all the overweight, out-of-shape people. You had no choice; you either got into serious shape or you died trying.

"Are you staying in Monsieur Bernard's place?"

"I believe so… Do you know him?"

"*Oui*. I did not realize he was going away this month."

I hoped Monsieur Bernard was going away because I didn't care to share the accommodations with a stranger. Before I could shrug off the question, Étienne disappeared down the fifth-floor hall. As I pulled my suitcase up the last steps, I heard Rita's voice.

"Oh, I knew I should have called you myself to check rather than relying on Tatia. *Merci, monsieur.* I appreciate your being so gracious."

What?

Rita stood in the hallway, across from a frazzled-looking bald man who appeared to be in his late thirties. Étienne stood to her right, leaning on the suitcase and conversing with the man in French.

She turned to me as I approached, an anxious look on her face. "Anna, there's a bit of a mix-up with our reservation, but everything is okay. This is Benoît Bernard, our landlord. *Monsieur,* this is my sister, Anna Essex."

"*Bonjour, madame.*" He frowned, wringing his hands, and spoke again to Étienne.

"What is going on?" I asked Rita.

"He thought we were coming next month."

"You're kidding."

"I wish I were." Rita swiped her hand over her eyes. "He does not speak English, and I've been trying to communicate with him in what little French I know. It's been a nightmare."

"He says if you give him three hours," said Étienne,

"he will vacate the apartment and go to his home in Provence."

"Yes, I believe we had established that— Who is this?" Rita looked at Flirty French Boy as if seeing him for the first time.

"This is Étienne. He...he helped me carry my bags up."

"That's very nice of you, um—Étienne. *Merci*. I'm Rita, Anna's sister."

They shook hands and I noticed that Flirty French Boy did not kiss Rita's hand. For some absurd reason, I found that satisfying. And then I felt ashamed of myself for being so ridiculous when there were more pressing issues at hand—such as whether Rita and I had a place to stay for the next ten days.

"You speak English very well," Rita said.

Flirty French Boy gave a smug nod, his mouth puckered in self-satisfaction. So very French.

"Would you mind translating what I say into French for Monsieur Bernard?" Rita asked.

"It would be my pleasure."

"Please ask *monsieur* if he would mind letting us leave our bags here for the time being, while we get out of his hair?"

My stomach lurched and my eyes darted to the green monster. Flirty French Boy had finally relinquished his grasp on it and it sat propped against the wall adjacent to Monsieur Bernard's door. The smaller bag leaned against it, as if exhausted from the long journey across the sea and the bump-and-scrape adventure five flights up.

Étienne scrunched up his face. "What do you mean, *out of his hair?* I do not know what you mean."

Rita laughed.

"Rita." I grabbed her arm and shook my head.

"Oh, you're right, I should watch my slang. I mean we want to leave the bags here while we allow him to—"

"Rita, no! Come over here for a minute." I jerked my head in the direction opposite of Étienne. "I need to talk to you."

Rita frowned at me. "Excuse me."

I tugged her down three steps, a good enough distance to talk privately if we whispered.

"What are you doing?" I asked.

"I should have called before we left, but I took it for granted my assistant, Tatia, had arranged everything. There must have been some kind of communication breakdown, because he was expecting us this time next month. But isn't it great of him to vacate the place for us?"

I looked up to see Flirty French Boy staring down at us, and I turned my back on him, stepping in closer to Rita.

"Yes, it's very nice, but we can't just go off and leave our stuff here. We don't know these people. What if Monsieur Bernard takes off for his home in Provence with our things?"

"Don't be ridiculous. What are we supposed to do with our baggage for three hours if we don't leave it here?"

"Take it with us, I suppose."

The thought of hauling the bags down then back up again was not appealing, but it was better than turning over everything I owned—well, everything I needed for the next three months—to a man who was not expecting us, but kindly, miraculously offered to vacate on the spur of the moment. And he was helped along by this boy thief.

Gypsies. That's what these two men were. They were gypsies working together to fleece unsuspecting tourists out of everything but the shirts off their backs.

I hitched my purse up higher on my shoulder. If we went along with their flimsy plan we were setting ourselves up to be robbed blind.

In that case, we were even *more* naive than Shirley Valentine.

"I am worn out," Rita said. "You do what you want, but I'm not schlepping bags all over Paris."

She turned and went back upstairs. I followed her, arriving in front of Monsieur Bernard's door in time to see Étienne wheeling the green monster and family inside.

CHAPTER 6

I didn't want to spend my first day in Paris obsessing over luggage. Really, I didn't. I wanted to get out and walk in the sun. I wanted to celebrate coming this far.

I wanted to see the Eiffel Tower.

I wanted to see Paris.

So I shelved my doubts, compartmentalizing them in that tiny place in the back of my mind. I forced myself to have faith when Rita insisted Benoît Bernard and Flirty French Boy—she didn't say that, she called him Étienne—would *not* take off with our suitcases.

"Tatia knows Bernard. He's a friend of her family's. They go way back. If the place is all boarded up and our stuff is gone, Tatia will know where to find him. Okay?"

"This would be the same Tatia who reserved the apartment for *next month*?"

Rita gave me a look before she walked out of the apartment building's dark vestibule. I followed her out into the sunlight bathing the rue de l'Ancienne Comédie. That expression didn't grace her face very often, but I knew it meant she wasn't in the mood to argue.

I took a deep breath and let simmer the prickly sensation needling me to bicker.

She was right. I was being an anxious idiot for worrying. But when you're so tired you can't see straight, sometimes the obvious looks a little off-kilter.

She wanted to go to the Musée Picasso. She said it was the only thing she wanted to do; if we could just get it out of the way first she'd do whatever I wanted.

We walked in silence, the turbulent morning sending us into our respective shells. When we got to the museum, housed in the former mansion of the Lord of Fontenay, we went our separate ways, viewing the collection solo, at our own pace.

That was okay. In fact, it was better that way. It would give us time to decompress, time to breathe.

If nothing else, the large house was magnificent. The entryway boasted an elaborate staircase adorned with sculptures. Picasso's work was arranged chronologically, starting with the self-portrait he painted in 1901 and ending with *Seated Old Man*, one of his last paintings, done in 1971. It was interesting to see the evolution of Picasso unfold right before my eyes, even if I didn't care for his work.

If I didn't know better, it felt as if I was actually beginning to understand where the guy was coming from with his Minotaurs and dead matadors and portraits of broken people quartered and drawn into geometric shapes.

It *must* have been the exhaustion speaking. I'd *never*

identified with Picasso before, except for that brief moment of insanity when I painted the hideous blue portrait of Blake.

O'Keeffe was more my style. Because my style was all about curves, flowers and blooming possibility. Yes, possibility, despite everything.

Imagine that.

Obviously, the flowers worked since they won me a ticket to Paris.

Picasso was all about cubes, flat, hard angles and grotesque distortion. His body of work contained exceptions to this rule, of course, but monstrous, misshapen, hard lines were what I thought of when he came to mind.

As I stared at the *Portrait of Jaime Sabartés* that he painted in 1939, the way he angled the glasses to the right and had the subject's nose pointing off the left side of his face, it looked as if someone had been so mad at poor Jaime they'd slapped him. Perhaps Picasso caught him the split second the blow displaced his features. Just as in my mind's eye, the angry rage that gripped me over Blake's duplicity conjured the image of the blue two-headed beast.

From the little I knew about Picasso, he was so disagreeable, he probably would have disdained anyone who *identified* with his art, or worse yet tried to attach meaning to it. But wandering the galleries in the old seventeenth-century mansion, I floated in a dreamlike state and felt a kinship I never knew existed. Especially when I happened upon a plaque that translated:

Painting isn't an aesthetic operation; it's a form of magic designed as a mediator between this strange, hostile world and us, a way of seizing the power by giving form to our terrors as well as our desires.

When I came to that realization, I knew I had found my way.

—Pablo Picasso, 1946

A message.

Right.

But it was a nice thought, a nice quote, a serendipitous hook on which to hang my confidence as I ventured forth to make art in this city in which so many great artists had come before me.

I wandered into the last gallery, one I almost skipped because, according to the guidebook, it housed the work of a nineteenth-century female artist I'd never heard of, not to mention, it was getting close to the time Rita and I had agreed to meet. But I popped in for a quick look around before heading back downstairs.

The collection of pastel portraits captured me at first glance. They were both bold and understated at the same time, like Toulouse-Lautrec, only more human. The portraits captured people in out-of-the-ordinary ways—exaggerated shadows and colors. The work was extremely feminine, yet amazingly, for a nineteenth-century female artist, it spoke volumes about her independence, unheard of for a woman of that era. I studied the faces for a long time, trying to figure out how the artist, Camille Deveau, had accomplished such a feat.

Interesting that her work was housed in the same museum as Picasso. It was such a contrast to his.

I was so caught up in the anomaly of her work compared to Picasso's, or perhaps the slight similarity to my own, I stayed much longer than I should have. As I turned to leave, I noticed an old black-and-white photograph hanging on the wall near the door. I must have missed it when I entered.

The photo was of Deveau and her family. Something about the expression on her face gave me an odd sense of déjà vu, an almost out-of-body sensation, and I had to blink to ward off the unsettling feeling.

It was past noon when I finally met up with Rita.

"I thought I was in the wrong place," she said. "I was about to come looking for you."

"I'm sorry. I was swept away by the exhibit upstairs. Did you see it? Her name is Camille Deveau. Interesting, I've never heard of her. Have you?"

Rita shook her head. "I got swept into the gift shop. I just love museum shops."

She smiled and I was glad she wasn't irritated with me for keeping her waiting.

"Her work is lovely. Portraits. They have a haunting quality."

"Sorry I missed it," she said. "How about some lunch?"

"Sure, let's just start walking and see what we can find."

Outside of the museum, the air was cool and the sun shone bright in the cloudless sky. A perfect day for walking. Much better than the unrelenting Florida heat.

"I wish I could have stayed longer," I said. "There was a whole wall of Deveau's paintings I didn't get to see."

"You should have said something before we left. We could have gone back."

I shrugged. "That was fine for today. Perhaps we can go back another day."

"Sure we can," said Rita. "I'd like to see her work."

As we walked, Rita flipped through her guidebook, reading me interesting facts about the Marais quarter, which translated to swamp. "Once the neighborhood of royalty and noblemen, the place descended into an architectural wasteland after the French Revolution. In the 1960s the government recognized its historical significance and began restoring it."

We strolled the narrow, winding streets past chic galleries and boutiques, *boulangeries* and cafés, the stylish and fashionable shops incongruent with the splendid seventeenth-century mansions that once housed French nobility and their mistresses. When we got to an intersection I realized I was looking at everything but not really seeing. My mind kept floating back to the photograph of Camille Deveau. The same unsettled feeling of displacement engulfed me again.

I reminded myself to breathe and tried to let the

charm of the old blending with the new weave a spell that would take my breath away, just as I'd always dreamed it would. The scents of lavender and perfume soothed me. They lingered in the air, mingling with the sweet smell of the flower shops and savory aroma of baking bread, fried onions and garlic.

So much to take in—the sounds, smells, sights, all that history. I looked down at the ancient cobblestone street beneath my feet and wondered if perhaps Napoleon or Marie Antoinette had walked this path, or if Camille Desmoulins had trodden this passage on his way to the Palais-Royal before shouting "To the Bastille!"

It was like faking an orgasm.

I kept waiting for it to take my breath away. I kept thinking I should be *so* happy. I kept telling myself, I am in *Paris*. It was supposed to be love at first sight with this city. *What's wrong with you?*

A haunting sort of melancholy, a longing for something familiar gripped me. I glanced over at Rita and felt ashamed when I realized the sadness stemmed from missing Blake. She was not the person I was supposed to be strolling these streets with. In my dream of *Paris love at first sight*, Blake was supposed to be at my side. A second honeymoon where we walked hand in hand along the quays and he kissed me on the banks of the River Seine.

He was not going to spoil Paris for me because he did not deserve my sadness.

Rita did not deserve my ungratefulness.

So right there in the middle of the Marais, I'd made up my mind. I would snap out of it.

All right, so I did the best I could. Complete transformations took time.

"You know what I *really* want to do?" A new sparkle danced in Rita's eyes, which made me feel better. "For our first meal in Paris, I want to find a little café where we can sit outside and dine on *jambon et fromage* sandwiches on those thin, crispy baguettes. Mmm…I can taste it now."

"Ham and cheese?" I smiled at her, feeling a little more like myself again. "You really want to be a tourist today."

"*Oui, madame.*"

"All right, I'm with you, but I have a special request. As long as we're being tourists, let's go all out and go to the top of the Eiffel Tower. The Delacroix Centre is over there. I can check it out, see where I'm going to live, and we can eat ham-and-cheese baguettes and act like first-class tourists atop *la Tour Eiffel.*"

After looking at the map, we decided the walk, which would take us from the right bank to the left, was too far to attempt. So we decided to take the metro. We walked down to the rue Saint Antoine, bought a ticket at Bastille and picked up line number eight toward Balard. The train wasn't very crowded and we sat on the first seats inside the door. As the metro pulled away, a man started playing an accordion and a woman began singing "La Vie en Rose."

The performance was so hokey, it was priceless. First-class catering to the tourists. Wasn't that song quintessential Paris?

But as I glanced around the car, most of the riders didn't seem to notice—a young woman sat with her eyes closed listening to her MP3 player, a businessman worried his mustache as he studied the contents of a file, an older woman read a book.

Rita and I were probably the only tourists in the car. I put a euro in the singer's cup, which brought renewed energy to the middle of the song she was now singing for me.

"Don't pay them," Rita whispered. "Metro buskers are like stray cats. If you pay attention to them, they'll never leave."

I glanced at the woman. She smiled and redoubled her efforts, thrusting the cup at me again.

I lowered my gaze to Rita's tour book.

"May I see that?"

I took the guidebook and opened it to the colorful metro map. It reminded me of a picture of a child's game of pick-up sticks, with some of the pieces bent into strange trajectories.

Rita figured out our route from the Marais to the seventh arrondissement. She'd mastered the metro on her last trip to Paris. I hadn't even been on an American subway. If I was going to have any sort of life in Paris, I knew I'd better learn to read the metro map *tout de suite*.

"How did you know this is the right train?"

"We're here. We want to go here." She gave me a quick metro lesson and had me track the stops until we reached the École Militaire stop.

"I have a feeling you're going to use this metro station a lot," said Rita. "Get familiar with it."

On the platform, the air smelled faintly of urine, body odor and cigarette smoke. There was a man sitting on the ground near the exit steps strumming a guitar.

We made our way up and out into daylight, winding through the streets, passing dozens of red-canopied cafés and people rushing here and there, until we stood in front of the wrought-iron gates that led into the Delacroix Centre. Beyond the stately black grillwork, lush trees and flowers framed a winding stone path. It had the aura of a secret garden. I had a sudden rush of anticipation. Or was it foreboding? I couldn't tell the difference. All I knew was this was real.

In nine days Rita would leave me here and I would be on my own. The thought made me light-headed.

"Shall we go in?" Rita said.

As I thought about reaching out to open the gate, contemplated taking my first step into the courtyard, a couple approached the gate from the inside and I stepped back to let them pass.

A stunning couple, he was tall and broad-shouldered with longish, dark, unruly hair and a shadow of unshaven beard. His black shirt, jeans and work boots were spattered with a substance that looked like plaster.

A member of the exchange program?

She was a tiny blonde with long thick, stick-straight blunt-cut hair that hung down to her waist. The kind of hair I used to dream of. Something in her swollen lips and tiny nose, or maybe it was her eyes—something about her reminded me of Brigitte Bardot.

The couple stopped outside the gate and she spat words at him so venomously it seemed she could have poisoned him with her tongue. All in French, of course, so I had no clue what she said.

He made a *pffff* sound and walked on a few yards, leaving her where she stood. She yelled something after him. He stopped, turned around and answered her, gesturing with both hands. He seemed more exasperated than angry as he raked both hands through his hair, made a little growl, staring at the heavens for a few beats before turning and walking off.

She hurried after him, her impossibly high heels clicking on the sidewalk. I couldn't fathom how she could run in heels and a pencil skirt.

"What was that?" Rita said.

I shrugged, watching the blonde catch up to him before they disappeared around a corner.

What a gorgeous couple they made. He was so big and so…so French. If he was French, he probably wasn't part of the exchange… Well then, what was he doing at the center besides fighting with his wife or girlfriend, or whoever she was?

Even when Blake and I fought, there was never that

much fervor in our battles. I couldn't help but wonder if they made up as passionately as they fought.

The voyeur in me wished I knew what they were saying, but I didn't, which was a reminder that living in Paris would be a challenge.

I could learn.

I'd have to learn.

I stepped back from the gate. "I don't think I want to go in. Not right now. I just wanted to see it. Get familiar with the area. Let's get some lunch, climb to the top of the Eiffel Tower and then go back and see if your Benoît Bernard is ready for us."

"Are you sure?"

I nodded.

"Okay, we'll come back again another day. But, hey, watching them fight reminds me…" Rita rummaged in her purse, and pulled out a small bag. "I got you something at the Picasso museum."

Inside was a small refrigerator magnet that said, Painting is not done to decorate apartments. It is an instrument of war.—Picasso

The view from the Eiffel Tower's top observation deck was the only aphrodisiac one needed to get in the mood for Paris. From one side the view stretched across the green lawn of the Champ de Mars to the palatial École Militaire. On the other side, the Seine lay like a moat in front of the Trocadéro. It was all there. Paris in panorama. One need only make the effort to look, and if a person couldn't get in the mood up there, well, I suppose she had no business being in Paris.

I was in much better humor as we headed back to the apartment. Benoît Bernard was waiting for us. His bags were packed; ours lay untouched, right where Flirty French Boy deposited them. We paid Bernard ten days' rent and he gave us the keys.

Voilà. The worst was behind us.

I should have felt silly for making such a fuss, but I was too exhausted. Rita and I retired to our separate bedrooms and napped for the rest of the afternoon.

I awoke to the sound of someone knocking on the door and Rita's subsequent, "I'll get it."

Still groggy from deep sleep, I lay on the bed staring out the window at the golden glow the setting sun cast on the white building across the way. The morning's events seemed like a strange dream, and I was happy to awaken from it. I stretched and felt the delicious pull of the move all the way down to my toes. Coming out of the stretch, I noticed the pamphlet I'd picked up at the Picasso museum lying on the nightstand and I picked it up to look at it.

"*Bonsoir, madame.*" The familiar voice carried down the hall into my room, penetrating the closed door.

Flirty French Boy. What did he want? I paged through the pamphlet until I came to a small paragraph about Camille Deveau.

"Good evening, *monsieur.*" Rita sounded way too cheery.

How long had she been awake? "Étienne, right?"

I stopped reading. What was with this *monsieur* business? He was a *boy*, not a *monsieur*. I'd have to school Rita on the difference.

Come to think of it, I wasn't exactly thrilled about being called *madame* every time someone addressed me. It felt like a dressed-up version of *ma'am*. Being called ma'am made me feel old. I suppose the alternative *mademoiselle* would have been a little creepy, because *mademoiselle* was for a girl. Or for someone Flirty French Boy's age.

"I told Monsieur Bernard I would check to assure you were comfortable."

My gaze skimmed the paragraph telling about how Deveau was a proper nineteenth-century lady who came from a wealthy family, but defied convention to paint.

"Thank you," said Rita. "Would you like to come in?"

Oh, Rita, no. Don't encourage him. I put the brochure aside and snuggled deeper into the comforter.

"Annabelle is asleep," she said. "We're a little jet-lagged."

"*Merci, non.* I will not intrude. I just wanted to inquire that you have everything you desire and bring you these crêpes for your enjoyment. They're from my restaurant downstairs."

Did he say *his* restaurant? His as in *he worked there*, or his as in *he owned the place*?

"Thank you." Rita said. "I was just going to wake Anna so we could discuss dinner plans."

"I would offer to escort you to dinner, but I must work tonight. The evening hours are always busiest."

"Have you worked there long?"

"It is a family business started by my great-grandfather. You must try it sometime, but on your first evening you should have a special meal. I recommend Le Bosquet."

He gave Rita the restaurant address and said, "For authentic French food, it will not disappoint. Perhaps tomorrow evening you will allow me to show you authentic Paris? It would be my honor."

Say no! It was awfully nice of him to offer, but—

I sat up and contemplated going out there and telling him thanks, but no thanks. But I caught a glimpse of myself in the mirror and saw that my hair was a little too unruly and I was in my underwear. And the thought of going out there and telling him no was more terrifying than just letting him show us *authentic Paris*.

It wasn't as if he was trying to pick us up.

"I shall pick you up at nine o'clock tomorrow evening, *oui?*"

So he was picking up, in a different sense of the word.

I laughed out loud because the play on words was so ridiculous.

Looking at myself in the mirror I thought, *Get over yourself. You should be so lucky as to have a young French guy try to pick you up.*

I dressed to the sound of Étienne bidding Rita *adieu*. When I was sure the coast was clear, I ventured out of my room and found Rita in the kitchen inspecting the crêpes.

"You just missed your boyfriend."

She scavenged through the kitchen drawers until she found a knife and fork.

"My boyfriend? Sounded to me like he made a date with you."

She cut into what looked like a ham-and-cheese crêpe and took a bite. "You were eavesdropping?"

"You were right there in the hall. I couldn't help but hear."

"Then why didn't you come out and say hi?"

"Because you were doing just fine by yourself."

"Mmm, this is good." She took another bite. "He's very cute, you know."

"He could be my son."

"Really? No, he must be at least twenty-five. You would've been—"

"I'd be furious if Ben came home with someone closer to my age than his. The standard goes both ways."

"If Étienne's twenty-five, you would have been sixteen when he was born."

Ignoring her, I took a glass from the cupboard and drew some tap water.

She gestured at me with the fork. "I think you need to find yourself a lover while you're here, and if he's sixteen years younger, all the better. There's a bigger age difference between Demi and Ashton."

"I am not Demi Moore."

"He likes you." She leaned on the counter and took another bite of crêpe. "Look, he even brought you a gift of love from his family's restaurant. In some cultures that would be a marriage proposal."

"Oh, great, just what I need, a marriage proposal when I'm not even divorced yet. And if he brought the crêpes to *me*, why are *you* eating them?"

"Here…" Rita held out the foil with the remnants of the feast. Semicongealed white cheese oozed out of a delicate pancake. "Have the rest. It's delicious."

I took it from her, tasted the remains.

"Good, huh?"

"Mmm." I forked another bite.

Rita unwrapped the other foil, stuck her finger in and tasted the dark sauce. "Oh my God… Chocolate…and orange. This has to be Grand Marnier. *I* would sleep with Étienne for Grand Marnier crêpes."

"You're too easy. And what will you tell Fred?"

"Fred who?"

Étienne called promptly at nine the next evening just as he'd promised. In-line skates dangled from his shoulder.

"What's this?" Rita asked, eyeing the skates as she showed him into the living room.

He smiled at me and waved. He looked like a little boy. "I thought you might want to see the real Paris by night."

"That sounds nice," I said. "But I'd like to live to tell about it."

Étienne laughed. "You do not skate? Everybody in Paris skates."

I shook my head. I'd never tried in-line skating. "No, the woman I saw coming out of the Chanel boutique yesterday was definitely not wearing in-line skates. Not *everyone* skates. Sorry, French Boy, I'll pass."

I looked at Rita for backup, but she just gave a non-committal shrug and busied herself.

Étienne scrunched his face into a mask of consternation. "I beg your pardon? French Boy?"

Oops. I didn't mean to hurt his feelings.

"Sorry. *Étienne*. Look, it's very sweet of you to offer to show us around, but I know my limits. This body is not primed for skating."

He looked me up and down, his gaze lingering unapologetically in *certain* places before returning to my eyes. "American Woman, I think your body is fine. "

Did he just call me— "Did you call me American Woman?" I laughed and so did he. I liked this kid. He was fun.

So we settled on watching the skaters who gathered at the base of the Montparnasse Tower, then we decided to explore the area and get a bite to eat.

It was a little awkward letting him lead us around Paris, but we did. It was also a little disconcerting when each time I'd glance at him I caught him staring at me—he had this piercing, unwavering gaze that kind of gave me the heebie-jeebies.

At one point while we rode a particularly crowded metro, sharing the same metal pole, he reached out and fingered a piece of hair that had broken free from my chignon. I pretended not to notice.

I was wedged into a cramped space just inside the door and had nowhere to move. A smelly man clung to the pole directly in front me, a row of occupied seats blocked me from moving to my right and Étienne stood to my left. Rita was on the other side of him looking all around, taking it all in. I tried to catch her eye, but she was too busy people watching.

So as I stood there hanging on to the pole thinking of that song by the Police, "Don't Stand So Close To Me," I brushed the errant piece of hair back as if his hand weren't even there then leaned in and said, "Look at Rita."

Étienne glanced over his shoulder, then smiled back at me. "She is *obiblious* to us watching her."

"She's what?" I thought he was mixing French and English and I wanted to learn as much of the language as I could.

"She is *obiblious*."

"*Obiblious?* What does that mean?"

He looked baffled. "*Obiblious*. It is an English word, no? It means to be unaware."

"*Oblivious*." I couldn't help it. I laughed and hoped that my French blunders would be half as adorable as his English mistakes. *Obiblious*. Ha! Cute.

The brakes squealed as the train slowed down to

enter a station. The force pushed him into me. He steadied himself with a caressing hand on my shoulder.

A sweet gesture, but a little too familiar for my comfort zone. When the doors opened and a woman vacated the seat in front of me, I took it, relieved to regain some of my personal space.

As I sat there, glancing up at Étienne occasionally, I wondered what was wrong with me. Why didn't I want to lean into him and flirt back? Why didn't I want to call his bluff and see if the vibes he emitted were what I thought they were. He really was a cute guy.

Not that cute was the be-all and end-all.

Even if he had a *Shirley Valentine* hobby of picking up middle-aged women tourists, why not go for the thrill of a no-strings-attached foreign fling? A cute guy. Hot sex. It might be good for me.

The train rumbled on. Was it the age difference that bothered me?

I'd never been hung up on age.

I didn't mind being forty-one.

I didn't even flinch at turning forty.

What *did* bother me was how fast time had slipped away.

Yesterday, I was at the starting line, then all of a sudden the gun went off and life came at me so fast and furiously I didn't even have time for my head to spin.

I blinked and missed it. I'd slept away my youth and

NANCY ROBARDS THOMPSON   131

awakened to find myself in this foreign land called middle age.

I'd given Blake the best years of my life.

Now that I was free, this is when life really began.

Glancing up at Flirty French Boy, I decided I'd have to ponder my options.

We took the metro stop that allowed us to walk past Luxembourg Gardens and the Montparnasse train station before we arrived at the Montparnasse Tower. Étienne laced on his skates while Rita and I sat at a café table. He was like a kid restricted by grown-ups.

"Étienne, if you want to skate, please don't let us hold you up," Rita said. "We will be fine here."

He swirled to a stop and planted himself in a chair. "Absolutely not. You are my dates and I shall ensure you have a good time."

Rita and I exchanged a quick glance. *His mama raised him right.*

We ordered cappuccino all the way around. After the server left, I asked, "Do you have a girlfriend?"

He shook his head, watching the skaters gather en masse at the bottom of the Montparnasse Tower.

"Why not?"

He shrugged.

"A good-looking kid like you should not be out with two middle-aged ladies on a Friday night."

Rita kicked me under the table. A reprimand. *This guy's into you. Don't blow it.*

By ten o'clock the street was flooded with thousands

of people of all ages on in-line skates. It seemed as if everyone in Paris *did* skate. I watched in amazement as people older than I was rolled by. It was as if someone had opened the floodgates and let in all these people. Étienne sat next to me, rolling his skate-clad feet back and forth as if he was revving his engine.

It really did look like fun.

"Is it hard to skate?"

He shook his head. "I could give you a lesson." He was on his feet, trying to pull me to mine.

"One slight problem. I don't have skates."

"There is a skate shop right over there." He pointed somewhere over my shoulder. "We can rent you a pair."

I looked at Rita to see if she had any interest whatsoever in skating.

"I will if you will," I said.

Rita shook her head and waved me off. "Go on, though. Really. I'll be fine right here."

I tugged out of Étienne's grasp. "No. Not unless you do."

"Will you please get out there?" She smiled and pulled her cell phone from her purse. "I need to call Fred and then I'll enjoy the show sitting right here. Go on."

Étienne was already down on the street, motioning for me to join him. I knew it was insane. I'd probably fall and break my butt. With one last glance at Rita, I joined him and we walked down the block, dodging the skaters, to a skate shop where a friend of Étienne's fitted me with skates and head-to-toe gear.

Skating was easier than I thought. I fell on my rear end a couple of times, but I managed to pick up the basics quickly. It was similar to ice skating, which I'd done when I was a child, and it came back fast.

Soon Étienne and I were out in the thick of things, and I was feeling pretty proud of myself. Together, we rolled over miles of road, pacing up and down the streets of Paris until I was so exhausted I had to sit down.

"Come on, let's rest a minute." I landed hard on a wooden bench outside a tobacco shop. Étienne spun in a half circle in front of me to stop himself.

"You're a show-off, French Boy."

"I like how you call me that."

"What? Show-off or French Boy?"

He grinned. "French Boy. But shouldn't you say French Man?"

I considered it for a minute and shook my head. "French Boy. It suits you."

We sat quietly for a moment, watching the skaters stream by. "I started to ask you earlier. Why isn't a nice guy like you out with a girl his own age on a Friday night?"

He raised one shoulder to his ear. "I go where I want. I suppose I prefer the company of mature women to those my own age. You have more to say. Opinions."

Mature women. Ouch. At least he appreciates quality.

"Besides," he said, "I have a *crush for* American women."

A *crush for…* "Oh, you mean you prefer American women to French?"

He nodded.

"Usually we say I have a crush *on*. It usually relates to one particular person."

He watched my lips as I talked, occasionally lifting his gaze to my eyes. "Someday I would hope to *marriage* an American woman and move to the United States and open my own restaurant."

I forced myself not to correct him this time. His English was far better than my French. I'd be mortified if someone corrected my every other word of French. "You don't need to get married to do that."

"It makes it much easier if I am *marriaged, non?*"

Okay, I got it. *Shirley Valentine* wasn't his movie. It was *Green Card*. He was a young Gérard Depardieu in training.

"No, it doesn't make it easier. At least not in the long run." I looked at his soft baby face and shook my head. "French Boy, find a nice French girl your own age and get married for the *right* reasons."

My mind skittered to the night I told Blake I was pregnant and how he came to me the next day with the decision that we should marry. I wondered if he really didn't know he was gay when he proposed or if I'd just served a convenient purpose?

Étienne leaned and whispered in my ear, "I have a crush for *you*."

"I have a crush *on* you," I said.

He smiled and his eyes lit up, "Then you will *marriage* me? *Non?*"

CHAPTER 7

Even after I turned down his green-card marriage proposal, Étienne still hung around, bringing us crêpes from his restaurant and showing us off-the-beaten-track Paris. The time flew by.

Rita's last day arrived too fast. She had a three o'clock flight, and I would begin my residency at the Delacroix International Exchange Centre.

No more vacation.

No more sight-seeing.

Time to get to work, prove my worth.

Étienne took our bags ahead to the center so Rita and I could walk leisurely on our last day together in Paris.

"I'd like to get some lavender and olive oil to take back with me," said Rita.

"Let's go to the rue de Buci. There's an Olivier & Co. over there and lots of florists."

We walked past the corner café, which was crowded with revelers sitting under its red awning, sipping coffee and eating baguettes. We turned the corner and the market-street rue de Buci burst forth with color, scent and people. Stalls spilled onto the street from shops that lined the tiny road.

We passed a cheese vendor, a chocolatier, and I inhaled the mouthwatering scent of cocoa. It gave way to the fresh sea-smell of crabs, oysters and lobsters that crowded an icy bed at the fish stall, then to the tantalizing scent of espresso from an elegant *salon-de-thé*, and finally to the subtle aroma of fresh fruit from the corner produce stall.

And then there were the flowers.

The most beautiful flowers in Paris were on the rue de Buci, and while Rita ducked into the Mediterranean gourmet shop to buy her souvenirs, I strolled over to a magnificent flower stand.

Heaped in huge buckets, the blooms' sweet, exotic scent lured me into the shop. Reds and violets, blues, pinks and oranges, each blossom looked as if it were carefully crafted by hand, every delicate petal cut and shaped into the perfect bloom.

Three clerks helped customers. One arranged a bouquet of fresh spring flowers for a tall, slim, fashionable woman; another wrapped a spidery green plant for an elderly woman; and the third presented the unique creations the shop offered to a handsome man in an expensive-looking suit, probably Armani. She spoke too fast for me to catch a hint of what she was saying, but she pointed to each selection, which had hand-written tags bearing the names of the arrangements:

Le Bouquet Gourmand, which appeared to be Cézanne roses, freesias and other ruffly blooms in every shade of pink available, arranged in a basket large enough to carry to market once the blooms faded.

The man's upper lip curled and he shook his head.

Next, she pointed to *Soleils de Nos Jardins*, sunflowers, plain and simple, arranged into a cheery bouquet.

He eyed the offering and shrugged, a bored, borderline-disgusted look on his face, before finally shaking his head.

No to the market basket; no to the casual sunflowers; for whom would such a man purchase flowers at this hour of the morning...?

Next she offered *Le Bouquet Parfumé*, a cameo of red and yellow roses, carnations and freesias.

He shrugged again, but this time the gesture held more possibility. Ah, roses and freesias. Romantic. Must be a lover.

Finally she presented *La Multitude de Roses*—a bouquet of three dozen multicolored roses, surrounded by wispy foliage. A classic bouquet, full of charm and beauty, I imagined the woman saying.

The man pursed his lips and nodded, and the woman gathered perfect long-stemmed roses from large green tubs. Each of the rose tubs had cards bearing women's names. Carol, Blanche, Gabrielle, Isabelle, Sophie, Sabine...

"Bonjour, madame."

I turned to see a man at the counter peering at me from behind a dozen red-tipped yellow roses he was arranging in a crystal vase.

"*Bonjour.*"

He must have caught my accent because he immediately switched to English. "May I help you?"

"*Oui, s'il vous plaît.* I am looking for dried lavender."

He held up a finger. "Ah, *lavande, oui.*"

He disappeared behind a curtain. That's when I spied the bucket of roses named Annabelle right next to a bucket of white roses labeled Camille.

A double thrill, startling and pleasing, to find a rose named after me sitting right next to one named Camille, because it reminded me of Camille Deveau.

More than that, it was comfort, as if I'd found a friend.

The man in the Armani suit brushed past me carrying the large bouquet of roses by the stems, blooms down. Even though it seemed a grave disrespect to the delicate blossoms, the way he moved seemed like it must have been the correct way to carry the flowers.

To a lover, no doubt. Or perhaps an apology to his wife for staying overnight *with* the lover? No, they were for the lover, I decided, lifting one of the Annabelle roses to my nose.

It was a spectacular creamy soft pink with dark pink tips and splashes of hot pink on the outside petals. Just the rose I'd hope a lover would have chosen for me.

"*Voilà, madame.*" The florist returned with a generous bag of dried lavender, which I supposed was what Rita wanted to take back with her. I doubted she could get fresh flowers through customs.

With a pang of regret, I replaced the Annabelle stem in the tub and walked over to the counter.

"You would like some roses?" asked the shopkeeper.

"Yes, I would, but—"

I would love some roses and a lover to bring them to me. Étienne's face flashed in my mind. Thinking of him in the context of lover made me cringe a little.

So unfair to him. Some woman would be very lucky to have his attentions. He was just not for me. I was not ready for...for *anyone*.

The shopkeeper walked over to the cooler of roses and plucked out a stem of Annabelle. "You like?"

A wild thought rushed through me. Why wait for a lover to bring me flowers? Why not purchase them as a sort of *housewarming* present for myself? To welcome me to my new studio. A chill wound its way through my veins. Who better to take care of me than me?

"*Oui*. Annabelle is my name."

The shopkeeper smiled.

If I needed justification...I would paint them. The Annabelle rose, my first project.

I asked for a dozen Annabelles and one Camille (for the symbolism), and the shopkeeper threw in six additional Annabelles.

"Gratis." His gaze lingered for a moment and he arched his right brow. Heat spread through my cheeks and I dropped my gaze to his ringless left hand.

I was beginning to see a common trait among Frenchmen. For lack of a better word, I'd have to call it "the look." It was this sultry way they looked at you that made you feel beautiful and appreciated. Why was it that when the majority of American men looked at women it felt as if they were undressing you?

Just one of the many cultural differences.

"*Merci, monsieur. Au revoir.*"

"*Au revoir, madame.* Do permit me the pleasure of serving you again."

I carried my bouquet by the stems, blooms down, and met Rita, who was still browsing, at Olivier & Co. After she finished, we continued our journey toward the Delacroix Centre. Turning onto a quiet wisp of a winding cobblestone street about the width of a sidewalk, I gave her the package of dried lavender.

"Thank you." She stopped and hugged me.

A sweep of seventeenth-century buildings stretched above us as if waking from a sound night's sleep.

It reminded me of how I lay awake most of the night, contemplating that today I'd be on my own in this big city.

"I don't know what I'm going to do without you," I said. My eyes welled with a mixture of emotions—gratitude for my sister, fear for what lay ahead.

"Can't you just stay?"

My voice broke on the last word. Rita pulled back, holding me at arm's length. "You are going to be just fine."

Tears brimmed in her eyes, too, and for a minute I feared we were both going to lose our composure.

"There's always Étienne. The poor boy is smitten."

I rolled my wet eyes and we laughed together, right there, two sisters—two friends—standing in the gray shadows of the ancient buildings that were silhouetted by the early morning sun.

As we walked in silence, counting down the numbers to the Delacroix Centre, I buried my face in the roses and inhaled the sweet sent.

I didn't have to stay if I didn't want to.

I could get on a plane and go home.

My mouth went dry, and I desperately wanted another cup of coffee, perhaps with a couple of shots of brandy in it. But Rita didn't have time to stop. She wanted to get to the airport three hours before her flight, which meant she had to be there by noon. The drive took an hour, and by the time we found my studio, looked around the grounds a bit and gathered her luggage, it was nearly a quarter until eleven.

I thought about trying to convince her she didn't need to go quite that early, that we should stop and have one last café crème. But she was ready to go.

I couldn't blame her.

Since I'd learned of Blake's secret, she'd been there for me around the clock, even going so far as to fly to Paris to deliver me to the next chapter of my life.

She'd done more than one woman should be expected to do within the bounds of sisterhood.

I realized at that moment that when life felt as if it

was crashing down on me, all I had to do was focus on how blessed I was to have the gift of her in my life.

I wanted to tell her this. I wanted to somehow express how grateful I was for everything she'd done, but I couldn't articulate the words without losing my composure. So, after I hugged my sister one last time, I handed her one perfectly formed, long-stemmed pink Annabelle rose.

She reached in her bag and handed me a beautifully wrapped box.

"This is for your stay in Paris."

Her cab pulled away, and I wandered the center's gardens for a while before I made my way back to my studio to unpack and settle in before the evening's welcome reception.

The studios were small Mediterranean-style bungalows with white stucco walls and clay tile roofs. From what I gathered during my stroll, they were scattered randomly throughout the twenty-acre grounds, grouped in pairs or quads.

My studio sat a good distance away from the entrance, next to a larger bungalow situated across a brick walkway.

Mine had a bedroom and private bath, a small kitchenette and a large, open space that served as both living room and studio space.

What I particularly loved was the French doors on the back wall that opened onto a patio surrounded by a privacy wall.

Pretty darn nice, I had to admit.

They'd left a fruit basket, a wedge of Brie and a nice bottle of Côtes du Rhône on the middle of the small wooden café table situated outside the kitchenette. There was also a welcome letter from Jacques Jauvert, the center director who'd called me with the good news that I'd won the residency.

I was eager to meet Monsieur Jauvert, whom I'd already decided I liked, based solely on his choice of wine, cheese and *me*.

Since it was a little early in the day for the Côtes du Rhône, I set the bottle on the kitchen counter next to the present Rita gave me, and my roses, which I'd arranged in a pitcher I found in one of the cupboards.

I eyed the box. What in the world had Rita done now? She'd already given me an Hermès scarf. I couldn't imagine how she'd top that.

Carefully, I unstuck the tape and folded back the floral wrapping paper to reveal—

Condoms?

Oh my God.

Ten boxes of ten condoms.

What in the hell was I going to do with one hundred rubbers?

Rita had enclosed a note:

Have sex. That's what you're supposed to do with one hundred rubbers.

I laughed out loud—my sister knew me too well—
and contemplated opening the bottle of wine. But instead, I chose a pear from the basket and sat at the table
to read the rest of Jauvert's letter.

Along with an outline of basic rules and regula-
tions—work ethic, quiet hours, respecting others' privacy, procedure for receiving visitors, the end-of-
residency exhibit and the purchase prize, among other
things—was a list of the other artists participating in the
program.

Interesting bunch, the twelve of us: in addition to
me, there were two other women—a mixed-media
artist, Lesya Sokolov from Romania, and Mei Ling, a
photographer from Beijing; and a total of nine men—
two African men—a potter and sculptor; a guy from Argentina who did watercolors; and then there was the
delegation of European men—four painters, one pastel
artist and a metal sculptor.

I finished the pear and the biographies, and searched
for the thermostat because it was a little stuffy, but I realized the bungalow wasn't equipped with an air condi-
tioner.

Okay. Well, at least Paris wasn't as hot and humid as
Florida.

I threw back the shutters and opened the French
doors and casement windows, hoping to create a cross-
breeze.

That's when I saw them—or at least a fleeting
glimpse of them—the man and the blonde I'd seen

fighting outside the entrance when Rita and I came here our first day. He unlocked the studio situated across the cobblestone walkway from mine and they walked in.

That was *his* studio? Across from mine?

For some odd reason my stomach spiraled. I pressed my hand to my belly.

Oh Lord.

He left his front door open, as if he couldn't be bothered to close it, and I hurried to open the other window in my studio, hoping to catch a peek inside his quarters.

No such luck. His door was ajar at an angle that obstructed my view and he didn't open the windows. The gentle peal of wind chimes drew my eye up to the weathered eave above his door.

I stood rooted to the spot, staring at his studio as if I could will him to open the place for my viewing pleasure or will myself X-ray vision to see inside. Finally, I grew tired of staring at the water-stained white stucco facade, at the garden hose coiled under the window, at the blue bucket spackled with plaster and the faded red towel that looked as if it had been lying there so long it had been bleached by the sun.

So much for the "rule" that asked artists to keep their space tidy "for the visual comfort of others."

He appeared again and dumped a cupful of food into a small dish sitting on the ground outside his door.

The rules said no pets.

Yes, he definitely had the air of a guy to whom the

rules didn't apply. And for some reason that made me smile.

Judging from the lived-in look of his studio and the fat gray-and-brown tiger-striped cat that sauntered up and ate the freshly deposited food, the guy wasn't here on a three-month residency. His place had the kind of well-worn look that took a while to achieve.

I didn't remember if the brochure in my acceptance packet mentioned long-term residents. I'd assumed the words *international*, and *exchange* in Delacroix International Exchange Centre were literal.

I was beginning to suspect most Parisian rules were put in place simply to be broken.

I started unpacking the green monster, contemplating what I'd wear to the welcome reception that evening, when strains of music started across the way. The mournful voice of a woman singing what sounded like the saddest song ever written floated through my open windows. She sang in a language I couldn't place. Not French. No, it wasn't Spanish, though the flowery acoustic guitar sounded Latin. Perhaps it was an Italian ballad? But that didn't sound quite right, either.

As I hung up my clothing, the music evoked the uninvited wistful longing I'd fended off since I'd arrived in Paris. I shook off the haunting sensation that fluctuated somewhere between melancholy homesick and wistful displacement.

For some strange reason it called to mind an old poem by Robinson Jeffers that advised not to worry about hating yourself, but to love instead your eyes that can see and your mind for hearing music.

The first song faded into a second and he cranked up the volume.

So much for rule number two on the list asking us to respect the peace and "creative quiet" of the other artists.

At least he wasn't into AC/DC or some obnoxious rap band I couldn't even begin to name.

Tonight at the reception it would give me something to talk to my handsome neighbor about. I could tell him I liked his taste in music and ask him about the language.

Yes, it would serve as a nice icebreaker.

One of the self-help books I picked up after Blake left introduced me to the power of personal affirmations.

The theory was if you told yourself something—repeated it over and over—eventually it would come to be by virtue of your belief.

When I started getting a little nervous about the welcome reception, I went into the bathroom, stared into the mirror and did my daily half dozen.

"I, Annabelle Essex, am okay."

I looked at myself in the mirror, waiting until I stopped inwardly cringing before I moved on to the next one. It took a while with this one.

In a perfect world, I wouldn't need affirmations. I

would simply exude confidence like the perfume emanating from the women at the mall cosmetics counters.

Someday I would believe this bunk. In the meantime, I could dream.

"Just because Blake's life was a lie does not mean by virtue of association, mine was, too."

That one was a little more palatable.

"I loved him. I upheld my vows. I refuse to assume the blame for his screwup."

"I'm smart, talented and I suppose men might find me reasonably attractive—if they like small, thin, soon-to-be-divorced middle-aged women with wild, curly hair."

I reached up and pulled out the elastic that held my hair in place and shook it free. My curls sprang to life and I immediately quashed the urge to gather up the strands and tame them into submission. Maybe if I learned to love my curls. I bent at the waist, flipped my hair forward then back. The shoulder-length mass grew twofold in volume. I smoothed it down. *Let's not get carried away.*

I refocused and said my last affirmation.

"I have the rest of my life ahead of me.

"My future is a blank canvas that I can embellish however I choose. I will paint myself a new life."

The burning question was, how long did I have to repeat the damn affirmations before they took root?

I paired a black handkerchief-hemline skirt with a simple black tank, tamed my hair into a neat twist, and started out about five minutes after eight toward the Delacroix Gallery, which was located about midway between my studio and the entrance to the center.

The lights blazed inside the studio across the way and thanks to the light, I caught a glimpse inside. There was a table just inside the door with pieces of marble each about the size of a concrete block.

He must be a sculptor. As I started to walk away, I heard what sounded like the start of an argument. The blonde said something in a sharp, shrill tone; he answered in an equally short, escalating tone of voice.

Oh, great. I hoped I wasn't in for three months of bickering.

When I opened the heavy wooden door and walked into the gallery, the first thing I saw was two very young, very chic, Parisian-looking women—one blond, one brunette—talking to a short, dour-looking middle-aged man whose face seemed incapable of smiling. All three heads swiveled in my direction just as it registered that I was the first to arrive.

"*Bonsoir*," said the man.

"*Bonsoir*," I said in return.

The Parisian Barbies murmured *bonsoir* in unison, and stood perfectly coiffed and made up, holding their wineglasses by the stem, dainty pinkies extended. They regarded me as if they expected me to start performing tricks like a trained monkey.

"I am Jacques Jauvert and you are—?"

"Oh, I'm Annabelle Essex."

I extended my hand. Jacques Jauvert regarded it with expressionless eyes before giving it a limp shake.

"You are the first of the artists to arrive. You are so prompt. Would you care for a glass of wine?" Before I could answer, he snapped his fingers and said something in French to Blond Barbie, who fetched me a glass of white.

"*Merci.*"

She gave a curt nod.

I gathered punctuality was not a virtue around here. Another quirky difference between French and Americans? I should have waited fifteen more minutes—or perhaps a half hour—before leaving my bungalow. I hated functions like this, and being the first to arrive was excruciating. There was no turning back now.

"Make yourself at home, look around—the artist in the exhibit is a Brazilian. We shall start after everyone arrives."

Carrying my wineglass by the delicate stem à la Parisian Barbie, I wandered around the open space looking at the paintings, skirting twelve cloth-covered easels. I hoped they were examples of everyone's work. I'd love to see examples of the talent that landed everyone here.

I wandered around for about twenty minutes looking at the Brazilian landscapes before the others began arriving.

Was there some unwritten rule stating if the function

started at eight o'clock it was really code for eight-thirty?

I'd keep that in mind for future functions, so I wouldn't show up looking like the punctual American dork. I noticed the two women wandering around looking as lost as I felt and decided to be the one who reached out.

I tried to introduce myself to Mei Ling, the photographer from Beijing, who didn't look a day over twelve, but she didn't speak English and didn't seem eager to communicate. I couldn't blame her, because I didn't speak Chinese and didn't want to resort to a game of charades.

That made me hesitant to approach the others directly. Instead, I opted for standing back, trying to make eye contact with them.

I realized with a thudding dread that I was easily the oldest person in the bunch, with the exception of one of the European painters who made me look masculine.

Five of the men chatted as if they'd already gotten acquainted. All in all it was a rather icy mixer, with the majority focusing their attention on the art exhibition. Probably pretending to look occupied while secretly sizing up the others just as I was. I don't know why I thought we'd instantly become one big happy multicultural family. There was a one-hundred-thousand-dollar cash prize at stake. Money did funny things to people.

I looked for my neighbor, but he wasn't among the

fashionably late. Oh well, this was a working residency—not a social trip abroad.

I was glad when Jacques Jauvert began his opening spiel, which he repeated in English. The Parisian Barbie who'd brought me the wine served as a Chinese interpreter for Mei Ling, who was the only one in the bunch who did not speak French or English.

Oh, I got it. *Interpreter Barbie.* You could probably buy her in Toys "R" Us right next to Veterinarian and Hawaiian Hula Barbies.

"I hope each of you had the opportunity to read the biographies I supplied. I realize some of you arrived this evening. I would like to make introductions so that you start putting names with faces."

He scanned the room and his unflinching gaze fell on me. "I shall start with our punctual American, Annabelle Essex, since she was the first to arrive tonight."

I smiled, feeling vaguely embarrassed by his backhanded compliment.

"Madame Essex is a painter," he said. "Out of all of the exchange residents, I expect to see the most growth from her when each of you presents your end-of-residency show."

Excuse me? My mouth went dry. If the first was a backhanded compliment, this felt like a full-on slap. With every eye in the room trained on me, I didn't like being singled out as the one with the most growth potential.

Come on. I knew I had room to improve, but need he share it with the entire group of artists?

I tilted my chin up a little higher.

"In all the years I've headed the program," Jauvert continued, "I've never granted a fellowship based solely on one work of art. Until now."

With this slam, I lost all feeling in my extremities.

Well, except for my face, on which I felt the start of a slow, deep burn. Judging by the look on his face, I had the sinking feeling things were rushing from bad to worse.

"In the entire body of work Madame Essex submitted, only one slide caught my eye—a large portrait in which I could see subtle influences of Picasso. But a fresh take, mind you, and vastly different from the *pretty*, decorative little florals that comprised the majority of her work."

In my peripheral vision, the walls melted like a Salvador Dali painting and the magnitude of how alone I was in this foreign city snapped into sharp focus.

Then, just when I thought the evening couldn't get any worse, the brunette Parisian Barbie whipped the cloth off a huge blowup of my blue painting of Blake.

Why didn't someone just kill me now?

CHAPTER 8

I didn't come to Paris to prime canvases for three months. But I couldn't paint anything else. Not after Jacques Jauvert dragged my self-esteem—and my flowers—through artistic mud.

"...*pretty*, decorative little florals..."

I hated the way his upper lip curled when he said it. I'd never heard the word *pretty* sound so *ugly*.

How could he like that hideous blue painting of Blake? It wasn't even a painting; it was a—a rant; the visual equivalent of a betrayed lover's diary entry. I'd never been good with words. That's why I painted.

Now I couldn't even paint and with no TV, no stereo, no Internet or telephone—except for my cell phone, which I had to use judiciously because overseas calls cost a fortune—I was about to go stir-crazy.

Even if I could talk to Ben or Rita longer than our once-a-week "I miss you!" conversations, I couldn't bring myself to cry on their shoulders over Jauvert's disparaging remarks.

It was embarrassing.

I felt like the butt of some French joke; let's bring

over the stupid American and hold her up to pubic ridicule.

Let's prove to the Parisian art community she has absolutely no talent.

Rationally, I knew that was ridiculous. They wouldn't invest the money in me for the sake of a good laugh. I knew that and for a short while, it imbued me with enough will to attempt a "blue" portrait of Jauvert.

I mean, if he liked the one of Blake so much I'd create one just for him: the sour little director sucking on lemons, with his hand tucked inside his jacket, Napoleon style.

After several false starts, each of which I ended up priming over, I dropped my brush on the table.

I didn't want to paint. I wanted to be anywhere but here, stuck inside this studio. It was sucking all the life out of me.

This had been the bulk of my existence for three weeks, except for my daily trips to the market for nourishment and fresh flowers. Read: chocolate, bread, cheese, fresh fruit and vegetables, wine and coffee for the new French press I'd purchased as a going-away present for myself before I left.

One of the pleasures of being on my own was this new freedom to eat how I wanted when I wanted. My daily trips to the Parisian markets were just about as close to heaven on earth as I'd ever find.

But back at the studio, it was hell.

That's when I realized I had to take a real field trip

or risk going crazy. I grabbed my jacket and decided to get the hell out of the studio before I went insane.

As I set out, I noticed that the sculptor's studio was shut up tight. At least one person in this place hadn't witnessed my humiliation that first night.

Subtle influences of Picasso, my ass.

I decided to go back to the Picasso museum. Just as I had declared a kinship with him on that first jet-lagged day, today I intended to divorce myself from his influence now that I was acclimated.

I wasn't a cubist painter. I didn't intend to copy his style, it just sort of erupted onto the canvas in a fit of cathartic expression. I was beginning to regret ever painting the portrait.

I accepted this residency intending to paint flowers, and if Jauvert and his board of critics expected more cubist distortions… Well, I just didn't have it in me.

At the museum, I stared at the key Picasso works that had moved me on that first day. But when they failed to spark any sort of feeling, I decided to go upstairs and visit Camille Deveau. I mounted the staircase and made my way up to her gallery, but her work was gone, replaced by an exhibit of contrasty black-and-white photographs.

I looked around as if they'd simply moved Deveau's work and I'd discover them behind me, but all I saw was photographs of the American West à la Ansel Adams and a docent slumping on a little stool next to the door.

"Excusez-moi, monsieur," I said. *"Parlez-vous anglais?"*

"Yes."

"The exhibit that was here before, Camille Deveau? Where did it go, *s'il vous plaît?*"

He scratched his bald head. "It ended three days ago. Next, it travels to Italy."

Disappointed and mad at myself for putting off a second visit, I wandered around the old mansion a little more until I finally found myself in the museum shop. Like Rita, I'm a sucker for museum gift shops. I can't get enough of all the little trinkets and art books and postcards. No matter how inaccessible the artist's work, the gift shop always managed to bring it to a human level.

I had just turned to leave, when a small book on the counter near the register caught my eye: a beautiful little biography of Camille Deveau.

I bought the book and took it to the Jardin des Tuileries, to a garden café situated under a thick canopy of trees just down from the Louvre.

The place crawled with tourists, people of all nationalities—lovers sipping wine in the afternoon; parties dressed in shorts and sneakers with cameras dangling from their necks, relaxing under the red umbrella tables after a morning of sight-seeing; others huddled together in close groups, posing for photos to preserve the memory of their time in Paris.

I chose a seat near the open building and sat down alone. Not a local, but not a tourist. Merely a stranger not particularly welcome in this strange land.

* * *

One of the things I love about Paris is that when you sit down at a café, there's no rush. You can sit there all day savoring your espresso or pastis. I did just that and sat at my little table under the canopy of trees reading Camille Deveau's biography from start to finish.

It wasn't until I closed the book and blinked at the thinning café crowd that I realized I couldn't remember the last time I sat uninterrupted and read a book from cover to cover.

Her biography read like a tragic novel: a woman ahead of her time. Painter of beautiful flowers. A great talent gone unrecognized and unappreciated.

Now, this was a soul sister I could relate to. Filled with the sad beauty of her story, I wanted to put what I'd read into context, give her an actual sense of place. I took the metro to the Latour-Maubourg Varenne stop, one exit before my usual, because supposedly, this was the area where Camille Deveau lived with her family—right off the rue de Varenne.

The Deveaus and other wealthy residents who formerly lived in the Marais (ironically, the area where the Musée Picasso now stood) moved to this area and built the aristocratic town houses in the Invalides district.

I walked along the boulevard des Invalides, across the street from the imposing Hôtel National des Invalides—in France a *hôtel* was not a hotel in the American sense, but rather a large home. This place was built in the seventeenth century to house wounded and homeless veterans. It was the cornerstone of the posh neighborhood all those years ago. Following a map in the book, I ventured off the boulevard and walked down the tiny rue de Varenne.

To my right was the Musée Rodin—though it wasn't actually the Musée Rodin in the nineteenth century, as Rodin was still a struggling artist, but the mansion was there. To my left were the town houses the book talked about. The road was so narrow it seemed I could stretch out my arms and touch the ivy-covered wall fronting the museum and the old houses. But I stayed to my right so that I could get a better feel for the houses. I wanted to try to guess which one was hers because the book didn't say.

It was just a game. I knew it was. But what was the harm? If I squinted my eyes and blocked out the traffic noise coming from the busy street behind me, it was as if I'd traveled back in time.

I followed the stone wall until it gave way to a wrought-iron fence and I could see inside the grounds to a fabulous rose garden, home to hundreds of roses. My first thought was, *Oh, I want to paint them*, because I could tell from looking those weren't Gertrude Stein's ordinary roses, those were Parisian roses set against the elegant mansion in the background that stood as proud and stately in Camille Deveau's time as it did today. I turned around and saw the casement windows on the town house behind me.

The oddest sensation skittered through my veins, raising gooseflesh on my arms and the hair on the back of my neck.

This was it. This had to be where she lived. I paused and stared at the garden, the road, the old houses, overcome by the strange sensation I'd been here before. This was the first time I'd set foot on this street, yet there was something oddly familiar in the smell of the air, the narrowness of the old street, the courtyards and doorways.

I rubbed my arms and squeezed my eyes shut against the perplexing sensation pulsing inside me, but it didn't go away.

Blake and I once got into a debate over reincarnation. I loved the romantic notion that we'd all lived many lives—that death wasn't the end—and in those lives we gravitated to the souls who'd had an impact on us in the past.

"How else would you explain déjà vu?" I'd said.

"Maybe it's familiarity passed down through the genes generation after generation," he said. "A person's ancestors are Irish, so he's drawn to all that's Irish because it's in his blood."

Killjoy.

Just like Jauvert and his curled upper lip denigrating my "...*pretty*, decorative little florals..."

I gave the roses one last wistful look and turned back toward the boulevard des Invalides. The setting sun glinted off the Dôme Church that housed Napoleon's tomb and a cool breeze whispered through the trees lining the street. Cars whizzed by on the boulevard, setting me firmly in the twenty-first century.

* * *

I got back to the center just before dark, still feeling displaced but a little less alone thanks to my new insight into Camille Deveau's life.

Tomorrow, I'd go to the library—the *bibliothèque* (only the French could make a library sound like a nightclub)—and see what else I could discover about Camille. If I wasn't going to paint, I might as well do something productive.

I walked in the dark through the garden and up the winding path that led to my bungalow. As I approached, I saw lights on in the sculptor's studio. The same plaintive music I'd heard the first day I arrived—the last time I'd seen him at the studio—drifted through the open door and windows.

So did the soft sound of a woman laughing as I paused in the shadow of my dark bungalow and looked inside the open door of his studio. I had a better view tonight thanks to the lights on inside his place.

I caught a glimpse of him through the window. He wasn't wearing a shirt and a red bandanna covered his head. His chiseled features looked even more pronounced in the low light. Then he was gone.

Ominously sexy—were the words that sprang to mind.

He looked about my age.

He appeared in the window again, lighting a cigarette, and I turned around to act as if I was unlocking my door just in case he saw me.

But the woman laughed again and the musical lilt of her voice enticed me to turn around.

He wasn't at the window anymore, but I could smell his cigarette mingling with the faint scent of jasmine. He answered her in a sexy, low voice.

What were they talking about? None of my business, but I was still curious. They weren't being loud, but loud enough that I *could* hear them.

I don't know why I did it, but I walked closer to the window. Not right up to it, but to the edge of the shadows, just close enough to see the blonde standing stark naked in the middle of the floor—well, not stark naked—she wore a G-string and a pair of high heels. Naked enough.

The music hit a shrill, mournful note that made me back away fast—before I could see if he was naked, too, or register many details about his studio beyond the large marble sculptures.

Heat warmed my cheeks. That's what I got for peeping in windows.

As I unlocked my door—this time for real—and stepped inside, the blond woman's lyrical voice took an edge and before I could shut the door behind me, she was shouting at him.

He shouted back.

How vulnerable one must feel to fight when she's stripped naked—literally and emotionally.

I opened my windows—because the place was stuffy after I'd been out all day—and left my lights off. The couple fought for several minutes, so loud I was sure their voices must have carried over the entire compound, but no one came to quiet them down.

Then as abruptly as the shouting started, it stopped. I waited for one of them to storm out, but neither did.

The only sound was the woman on the CD singing her melancholy song. I shut the windows and latched the shutters, not wanting to hear how they made up.

Surely two people who fought so passionately made up just as passionately.

I didn't want to know.

Instead, I picked up my brush and put paint to canvas. Inspired for the first time since I'd arrived.

CHAPTER 9

If American women were truthful with themselves, they'd confess their envy of Frenchwomen, to whom style seems intrinsic and fat is something unfortunate that happens to other people.

They never have to loosen the waistbands of their tiny designer samples after polishing off a five-course meal, which includes, of course, large amounts of butter and cream, a cheese plate and something yummy such as crème brûlée or baba au rhum.

Their pouts translate to sultry and seductive to the male species.

They know how to wear scarves.

When I laid it all out, it seemed pretty clear that Frenchwomen had made a deal with the devil.

Oh well, my life had gone to hell.

I might as well join them.

Right. If only.

After staying up all night painting a scene I'd titled *The Bed*, depicting the passionate reconciliation of fighting lovers, I got stuck when it came to painting the woman's face.

The big white bed, heaped with sheets and pillows—
no problem. The *ominously sexy*, brooding man—no
problem.

The woman? Big problem.

Since Jacques Jauvert implied that my flowers were
an insult to Georgia O'Keeffe, I decided to borrow
Camille Deveau's bold portrait style. I'd come to a
standstill when I forced myself to drop O'Keeffe's meth-
ods. There was nothing wrong with borrowing someone
else's approach until I found my own way. It was better
than priming canvases.

My new line of attack was working. Except for the
woman's face, which I'd started and painted over at
least a dozen times.

I was tired.

At about nine o'clock in the morning I decided to
take a break. I considered getting some sleep, but I was
too keyed up to rest.

Instead, I flipped through *French Vogue*. I'd taken to
pretending it was a study guide to help improve my
French. I'd learned a lot, actually. I could translate the
Prada and Dolce & Gabbana ads.

So Prada and Dolce & Gabbana in French read the
same as they do in English. I was starting with simple
one-word ads and working my way up.

The Lierac Solaire self-tanner ad was what caught my
eye—the one with the bronze topless woman, lounging
as if she hadn't a care in the world. Before coming here,

I never considered myself prudish, but I had to admit, I wasn't quite as uninhibited as the average French-woman who thought nothing of parading topless—with the doors and windows open so that any nosy person who peeped in would get an eyeful.

Like Sexy Man's girlfriend across the way, who walked around his studio in her uniform of G-string and high heels. She moved as if she was so confident in her own skin she didn't care if the whole world was watching.

More power to you, honey.

If I had a body like hers, I'd walk around naked, too. Just because I could.

I just wasn't quite that…liberated.

So what did that make me?

A prude?

I didn't want to be a prude.

I tossed the magazine aside and got up off the couch, closed the shutters and walked to the bathroom mirror.

I slipped out of my jeans, and closed my eyes, trying to imagine myself sunbathing topless on the Riviera.

So glamorous. Such a deep, dark tan. No tan lines.

I opened my eyes and spied myself standing there in my shirt and underwear and the ridiculousness of it made me laugh out loud.

Why? What was so funny? Because I wasn't comfort-able with the thought of sunbathing topless?

Maybe I *was* a prude.

No.

If I got to the point where I was comfortable with my body, I could do it.

I undid the bottom two buttons on my shirt and lifted it, just barely, so I could examine my stomach.

My not-quite-flat-midriff hadn't seen the light of day since…. Since… Well, let's just say it had been a very long time. As I feared, I was frightfully pale. More than pale, actually. I edged the shirt up a little more. The white-fright factor conjured the word *fish-belly*.

How long *had* it been since I'd even had a tan? When I was a teenager, I used to spend most weekends at the beach and I looked great. But Blake hated the beach and had an obsessive fear of skin cancer. Plus, working nine-to-five and raising a son preempted the simple pleasure of sun-worshiping.

I pushed my shirt up under my breasts and did a quick turn and spied something even more horrifying than my pallid tummy: cellulite. On the back of my legs.

Holy shit.

Where did that come from?

I blinked at my legs, trying to imagine how I could shower daily and not notice the unsightly mess. Can we really go years without looking at ourselves? And how about that butt that didn't sit quite as high as it used to?

My focus snapped back to my legs.

I ran my hand over the mottled surface.

They were old legs. Tired legs. Unloved legs.

Dropping my shirttail, I walked out into the hall and

grabbed my jeans. But before I could dress, I spied the naked Lierac Solaire woman scowling at me from the *Vogue* ad as if she wanted to jump out of the magazine and slap me for being a disgrace to womankind.

"*You* don't have cellulite. Or a saggy ass. And you're not forty-one years old. I'll bet a man never left you for another man."

I kicked the magazine closed and stood glaring at it in the dim light.

"Don't let him make this your fault." I said the words aloud and a feeling washed over me until a voice deep down inside bubbled up to the surface.

"It's not my fault."

I went to the closet and retrieved the one and only pair of high-heeled sandals I brought with me—the ones I almost didn't bring because they were flirty and this was supposed to be a serious painting trip, but I ended up packing them because I had to bring something halfway fashionable. I mean, come on, it is Paris.

I slipped my feet into them. The leather soles felt cool. I took a step and glanced down and liked the way my ankles looked. I'd always had nice ankles. Thin ankles. And that was good, because not even a plastic surgeon could fix bad ankles.

Liposuction could fix cellulite, but pity the darling with fat ankles.

I walked in my high-heeled sandals and shirt back over to the mirror. I couldn't look at myself, but slowly, one, by one, I unbuttoned the shirt the rest of the way and shrugged it off, then I stepped out of my plain flesh-colored briefs and stood there until I could steal shy quick glances at myself.

Tears burned my eyes and I wrapped my arms around my middle.

"I, Annabelle Essex, am going to be okay," I said to the broken, vulnerable naked woman in the mirror. The words rang hollow, but a few seconds later, I noticed the woman in the mirror stood up straighter, with her shoulders back.

Maybe someday I'd have liposuction.

Maybe I wouldn't.

Maybe I needed to learn to love myself just the way I was.

Maybe I could use a little color.

I grabbed a towel, draped my big shirt around my bare shoulders and crept out onto the patio as if I were breaking and entering a quiet house in the middle of the night.

The morning sun shone bright, bathing the patio in gentle light. I hugged the towel to me as I surveyed the stucco walls, assessing the privacy factor. Satisfied that no one except the birds could see in, I spread my towel on the ground, slipped out of my shirt and sandals and lay down to soak up the sun—naked.

Naked as the woman in the Lierac Solaire self-tanner.

Nope. More naked. She was only topless.

More naked than the sculptor's girlfriend.

I lay there like that for the first time in my life deliciously soaking up the sun, loving the feel of it caressing my body…like a lover.

Mmm…yes, that was just the way a lover's hands should touch a woman's body….

I awoke to the sound of knocking at the door. My first groggy thought was, *Blake will get it.* I turned over on my side to snuggle into the downy softness of the mattress, but the bed was hard as a rock.

Hard as—

The knocking made me sit upright and grab for my shirt.

I'd fallen asleep.

Out there like this.

Naked.

I pulled on the shirt, buttoned it as fast as I could and stepped into my jeans, nearly falling over myself.

My heart pounded in a furious, deep-sleep-interrupted panic. As if I'd been caught doing something wrong.

I ignored the shame as I blinked away the haze and opened the door. Étienne was standing there holding a travel-size bottle of shampoo.

"*Bonjour, madame.*"

"*Bonjour*, Étienne. Don't call me *madame*. My name is Anna."

He glanced down at the shampoo, then lifted his gaze to mine. "*Bonjour*, Anna. Are you unwell? Your face is flushed."

I pressed my hand to my cheek and felt the warmth.

"Oh, no, I'm fine. I fell asleep out on the patio."

How much sun *had* I gotten? I glanced at my watch. Ten minutes after twelve. I'd slept for nearly three hours. No sunscreen. Great. From fish-belly white to lobster red in the span of a morning.

He held out the small bottle. "You left this in Monsieur Bernard's shower. I thought you might need it."

I reached out and took it. The motion caused the cotton shirt to rub across my bare breast and I was suddenly aware that I wasn't wearing a bra. I crossed my arms over my chest.

"Thank you for bringing it, Étienne. It must be Rita's, but I'll be able to use it."

An awkward silence ensued. I couldn't invite him in, the bed painting was sitting right in the middle of the floor—and I thought my underwear might be, too. I couldn't remember where I'd let it fall. I was just about to say goodbye when he said, "There is a festival happening today, La Fête du Pain. Would you care to accompany me?"

"Wait here just a minute."

I shut the door and carried the new painting to the patio. Silly to hide it, but I didn't want anyone looking at my work yet. I might even paint over the image. Although, at first glance, I liked what I saw. The partial image of the sculptor wasn't bad. It was coming along. I just needed to figure out what to do about the woman.

On the patio, I glanced up to make sure no rain clouds loomed. Not a cloud in the sky. The warm sun beat down through my shirt. The sting hinted at the severity of my sunburn, but I didn't have time to worry about it.

I shut the French doors, stashed my underwear in the bedroom and put on my bra. My sunburned breasts screamed at the invasion of elastic and wire, so I took it off.

I walked into the bathroom to inspect my bralessness in the mirror. The cotton shirt rubbed against my nipples and my nipples questioned the shirt's right to be there—over the bareness—since I was going out.

Thank goodness I wasn't overly endowed. Deciding I didn't look too obscene, I tied the shirt at the waist. Checked the mirror—yes, I could get away with this.

On my way to the front door to invite Étienne inside, I spied the empty easel. I don't know why I felt compelled, but I picked up a blank canvas and slid it onto the easel before opening the door.

It made it look as if I'd been doing *something*, or at least it looked like I was ready to do something. Étienne stood outside with one lanky arm braced against the doorjamb.

"Sorry about that. Come in."

He stepped inside. "So this is your studio? It is very nice."

"It's comfortable."

He walked around to look at the canvas on my easel.

Then he looked at the blank canvases lining the walls, primed but empty.

That made me feel silly for putting the blank one up there.

"You have been here three weeks. Where is the work you have produced? You have already sold it?"

"No, I'm going through my white, minimalist phase right now. If you'll look closely at the canvas on the easel, you'll see a tiny black dot right in the center. That's the painting."

Étienne squinted and leaned in for a closer look. Then glanced at me, looking confused.

"I'm kidding," I said. "Don't believe everything I say."

"Such as when you rejected my marriage proposal? I should believe you really meant yes?"

"Well, no. I was serious about that. I can't marry you. I'm married to someone else."

He knit his brows. "You told me you were single."

Why did I open that can of worms? "It's complicated, Étienne. I'm getting a divorce."

Frowning, he said, "Your husband is an idiot to let you go."

The look of conviction on his face tugged at my heart. "French Boy, I like you." I winked at him to lighten the mood.

"Then you will go with me to La Fête du Pain? Please, it is much fun."

"La Fête du Pain? That means bread celebration?"

He nodded.

How in the world could I resist an opportunity to pay homage to bread?

"At La Fête du Pain you will sample a multitude of fresh-baked bread. *Boulangers* will have ovens outside and will bake the bread before your eyes. A good friend of mine will give a special presentation at three o'clock. I told him I would stop by. And you could come and help me practice my English so that when I meet my American woman who will marriage me, I will be ready, *non?*"

He smiled his Flirty French Boy smile. I had to admit he was adorable. Still, babies and puppies were adorable, but I didn't want or need either. Nor did I want or need a Flirty French Boy in my bed.

He reached out and touched my hair again.

I could hardly convince him that I was in the middle of something important. The blank canvases spoke for themselves. And I'd admitted I was sleeping when he arrived. Yesterday, it did me a world of good to get out—

For the first time in weeks, I'd painted something worth keeping. Perhaps a quick walk through La Fête du Pain would continue that trend. To tell the truth, as luxurious as being a lady of leisure sounded in theory— spending the day doing nothing but reading a book; lying naked in the sun all morning; accomplishing nothing tangible—I needed to do something constructive with my time. Perhaps going out again, *Paris* would refill my well.

"It sounds like fun, but I can't stay long." Étienne dropped my curl and smiled. "*Oui*, I must work at three o'clock. But in this short time together I will be pleased to show you around. More of the real Paris, as you say."

Ah, the real Paris. Yes, there was that, too, and the bread. Wasn't bread the heart and soul of the real Paris?

"Have a seat while I change clothes."

I turned to go, but he grabbed my hand.

"*Non*, you look fine. I like your hair down that way."

I pulled my hand from his and touched my hair again, which I knew had to look wild after I'd slept on it all afternoon.

"Okay. Fine. Let's go."

As it turned out, La Fête du Pain was not just a huge Parisian bread festival, it was an annual event where bakers from all over Europe came to show off their baking prowess.

The plaza in front of the Hôtel de Ville (city hall) was covered with tents and wall-to-wall people. Large ovens had been set up for culinary artisans to display their expertise in rolling, dusting and baking breads of all types to crispy perfection.

The deliciously seductive aroma permeated the air and made me want to breathe deep. Étienne pulled me from tent to tent, elbowing his way to the samples, feeding me small morsels at each one. This one dipped in rosemary-garlic oil, that one spread with a particularly smelly cheese; yet another with a thin piece of pâté resting atop.

After we'd spent an hour stuffing ourselves with baguette, brown bread, challah and dozens more I couldn't begin to name, we watched his friend, Alain, who worked at the *crêperie*, present a demonstration on the fine art of crêpe making.

After Alain finished, Étienne introduced us. A stout man who looked to be in his midfifties, Alain kissed me on both cheeks and eyed me up and down in a manner that made me wish I'd taken the time to shower, apply makeup and dress properly for the occasion, rather than letting my wild hair fly free and tying up my big white man's shirt over my jeans. My flat sandals didn't help the ensemble, either. It didn't even cross my mind to put on my strappy ones.

Vive la différence between a Frenchwoman and me. Étienne and Alain talked in French. Rather than stand there dumbly not understanding what they were saying, I walked over to the baguette stand next door and took the sample an older woman offered. Less than a minute later, Étienne appeared at my side with a bottle of red wine and two glasses.

"One of the benefits of the business," he said, gesturing to the bottle. "Why don't we sit on the fountain and enjoy it."

We managed to squeeze into a tight spot that seemed better suited for one person than two. I was beginning to understand that Étienne's invasion of my personal space was not so…well, *personal*, as much as it was a cultural thing.

French people, Frenchmen in particular, were just more intimate human beings, more prone to touch and stand close to a woman than Americans.

Sitting on the edge of the fountain, with our hips and shoulders pressed together, we toasted La Fête du Pain and friendship, American painters and French crêpe chefs.

"This is so much fun." The wine numbed my nose, and when I smiled, my entire face tingled. "I am so glad you talked me into this."

Étienne moved his arm behind me so that his palm rested on the edge of the fountain. It opened a bit more room, but also angled him so that my shoulder pressed into his chest.

He smelled musky and earthy, a bit more pungent than I was used to. Some women thought a man's natural scent was sexy, but I'd always preferred the clean smell of soap and aftershave. Today, in the spirit of the festival, I vowed not to let it bother me.

"You are not used to having fun?" he asked.

"What?"

"Your American husband did not take you fun places like La Fête du Pain? No wonder you are divorcing him. He did not properly care for you."

Oh. Whoa. I realized I hadn't thought of Blake in at least two hours and the realization crashed in like a chandelier falling from the sky. I didn't want Blake to ruin this otherwise perfect day.

"I have been meaning to ask you," I said, changing

the subject. "Have you ever heard of a nineteenth-century French artist named Camille Deveau?"

He pursed his lips as if he was racking his brain, then shook his head.

"I hadn't either until that first day Rita and I arrived. We went to the Musée Picasso and there was an exhibit of her work. I went again yesterday to see it, but they had already taken it down. She was a really amazing person from the little I've read about her and I'd like to learn more. I was thinking about going to the library— um, to the *bibliothèque* to research her, but my French isn't strong enough to make much headway. Would you help me by translating for me?"

"Sure, you want to go now?"

I glanced at my watch. "It's quarter till three. Don't you have to work?"

He held up a finger. "Wait here. I'll be right back. One of the pleasures of being the boss is the—how you say—flexibility. I was to relieve Alain at the tent, but I will talk to him. I am sure he will not mind staying another hour. The *bibliothèque* is only open until four o'clock. We will go and do some quick research and then I will go to work and you will go home and paint."

The library was almost empty. After finding a couple of French reference books that mentioned Camille Deveau, we found a quiet corner table behind tall shelves. I set the books on the table, and Étienne glanced around and then pressed his finger to his lips.

"Shh, don't tell anyone." He pulled out another bottle of wine from the inside of his jacket.

"We can't—" What I meant was I couldn't. I was already half-drunk from the first bottle.

Another difference between the French and me— they could hold their wine. But Étienne had pulled out a chair for me on the same side of the table where he sat, opened the bottle and poured two glasses before my numb brain could send a message to my even number lips to say "We are going to get kicked out of here, if we don't get arrested first."

Étienne made a *pssssh* sound and handed me a wineglass, clinking his to mine. "This is not America. The librarian would probably join us if we invited her. As long as we don't spill on the books."

Leaning back casually in his chair, he propped his left ankle on his knee and his left knee pressed against my thigh. He sipped his wine and read to me from one of the books we found on the shelves. I sipped and listened, enjoying the melodic sound of his accented English, the warm glow of wine and sunburn and the way his lips moved.

He didn't seem so boyish sitting there next to me.

"The author speculates that even though there was no documentation—no journals or letters to prove it— Camille Deveau was the lover of Georges Fonteneau, the famous nineteenth-century painter. She draws this conclusion based on a series of portraits Fonteneau painted of Camille Deveau."

I drained the last of the wine from my glass. "I knew they were close friends, but I didn't know they were lovers. I mean, Fonteneau was married and Camille Deveau was a proper lady."

Étienne shifted forward to pour more of the ruby-colored liquid into our glasses and his knee pressed more firmly into me.

"So what do you think of your little artist now? Taking a married lover?" He touched his glass to mine and held my gaze. I was so caught up in the exotic color of his eyes—I'd never noticed the flecks of green mixed in with brown and amber.

I didn't even notice him leaning in, until his lips were on mine, softly at first, tasting of the wine—of black currants, spice, coffee and tobacco.

"I think she has the right idea," he murmured.

I was so taken aback that I didn't object. He deepened the kiss a few layers. My whirling mind registered my pounding heart and the velvet feel of his lips on mine—skilled lips, capable lips. Why did I think he was too young? Because, my God, he was just so darn good at this. So good at invading my personal space.

Vaguely, somewhere in the fuzzy background, I heard a female voice say, "Monsieur, Madame, la bibliothèque ferme dans cinq minutes." I think she said the library would close in five minutes.

The kiss tapered off with slow, hungry, smaller kisses. My vision was blurry when he finally sat back in the chair. I blinked him into focus.

"So you see, the librarian, she is *obiblious* to our drinking wine in here." He trailed his thumb over my cheek, down my neck to the first button of my shirt. A hot surge of lusty longing coursed through me.

And I thought I wasn't attracted to him. Give a starving woman bread and water and it tastes like a feast.

"You have to go to work and I better go home—or at least somewhere far away from you before I get into trouble."

He arched a brow. "You told me on that first day I met you that you have a fondness for trouble."

He stood and pulled me to my feet. I swayed, unsteady, and he wrapped his arms around the small of my back, placing biting kisses on my neck, pulling me to him and pressing his erection into me.

Heat stirred and pooled in my belly and my body responded in a way that begged me to lay him flat on the table and show him just how much I loved trouble.

Oh my God, what was wrong with me?

My head lolled to the side, reveling in the skill of his lips and hands and—I wobbled again, sidestepping into a shelf, knocking over the books on the end.

Oh my God, I was *drunk*. *That's* what was wrong with me.

I was drunk and I was making out in a public library with a boy who kept mixing up his words. I was like a schoolgirl. And I liked it.

It was a damn good thing we were in a public place

that was closing in the next minute or so because my body begged me to keep going.

"Let me come to you tonight after I quit work." Étienne's breath was hot in my ear.

If I let him we would probably... "No, we can't..."

His tongue was in my ear and he cupped my bottom so that my body was flush against him.

"Is this one of your noes I should not believe?" His hands traveled north and he unbuttoned my shirt, exposing my sunburned breasts, kneading them up and together like a skilled *boulanger*.

"Ouch, I'm sunburned." I tried to wriggle free, but he backed me against the shelf.

"I like it. It's very sexy, American Woman. You are not so much the uptight person as I first thought."

Just as his mouth ravaged one of my tender nipples, the librarian appeared at the entrance to our little alcove.

"Oh!" My gaze locked with hers. Pain mingled with ecstasy, which was nearly (but not quite) eclipsed by the horror of being discovered. All I could think was, *Oh my God, I should have worn a bra. I never go out without a bra.*

She pursed her lips, and as she walked away, I prayed she wasn't going to get security to throw us out.

The thought sobered me enough to realize library or no library, closing time or not, Étienne was going to keep going until he'd scored a home run. He slid his hand into my waistband, but I wriggled out of his grasp.

"Okay, French Boy, come on. It's time to go."

He stood there, breathing air in great gasps, his lips all wet and shiny, his hair mussed and his green shirt partially untucked.

As we walked to the metro on the crowded sidewalk, the traffic and harsh afternoon light curbed the lusty cravings that blossomed inside me in the library, leaving me feeling anxious and unsettled.

"I have to ask you something," I said.

"*Oui?*"

"How old are you?"

He knitted his brows and looked at me as if I'd asked him how many inches his penis measured.

"Why? Is that important to you?"

"Yes. It is. I usually like to know the age of the men I kiss."

He slanted me a perplexed sideways glance. "It seems irreverent to me. Because what is age but a chronological record of how long we have been on this earth?"

Irreverent?

"You mean *irrelevant?*"

He lifted one shoulder and let it fall.

"Okay, don't get all philosophical on me about age. Just answer my question."

"I am twenty-nine years last January."

It took my muzzy mind a few minutes to do the math, but I finally calculated the twelve-year age difference. So he was a few years older than I first thought, but he was still closer to Ben's age than mine. It made me want to ask what he was doing with *me* when any number of beautiful, young Frenchwomen—women much closer to his age—would line up for a man who could kiss like that.

Come to think of it, beautiful young *American* women would, too, and then he could have sex *and* get his green card.

We stopped at the entrance to my metro station. "Is this about the green card, Étienne? Because if it is, even when I get divorced, I'm not sure I ever want to get married again. Marriage is hard even when you do it for the right reasons. Don't marry someone just to get into the U.S."

He pulled me to him and ran his hands down the length of my back as he kissed me—right there in broad daylight at the entrance to the metro station.

I waited for the slow burn to ignite, but my body didn't respond the way it had before.

He pressed his lips to my ear and said, "*Non*, this is not about the green card. You do not need a green card for what I want to do with you."

His words made me blink and when he tried to kiss me, I turned my head to the side. He stepped back, looking a little insulted.

"Anna, I find you most attractive and I would like to be your lover. Does this trouble you?"

Did this trouble me? What a loaded question. Should I start with the age difference? Confess that despite my liking the *idea* of taking a younger lover, the reality was daunting; or did I tell him it had been eighteen years since I'd taken a lover and the man I chose ended up being gay?

Oh, no. No. I would *not* let the bad situation with Blake scare me away from healthy relationships.

It all came down to an issue of chemistry.

"Étienne, I'm just not…"

He looked down at me expectantly.

I sighed. "I'm still married and I guess until I sign the final divorce papers I just don't feel right about becoming someone's lover."

He looked at me as if I'd said something totally incomprehensible. I supposed since the two favorite sports of the French are eating and adultery, my reasoning for not being his lover sounded a little thin.

It *was* a thin excuse. But even though I responded to him when he kissed me—it had been ages since I'd had a man's hands on my body, so I think I would have responded if Quasimodo had ravished me. Not that Étienne was in any way Quasimodoish.

There was just no explaining chemistry.

"I will not force myself on you, but it is a shame that you let this man you are divorcing keep you from being truly free. Come to me at midnight, Anna, and I promise you won't regret it. I will work at the festival until six o'clock, then I will be at the restaurant waiting for you."

I opened my mouth to speak, though I don't know what I was going to say, but he dusted my lips with a feather-soft kiss.

As I watched his tall, thin frame walk away, I felt woozy and flattered and uncertain…and petrified all at once.

A good friend once said France would be lovely if not for the Frenchmen. Obviously, she hadn't been kissed senseless in the middle of the afternoon by a virile young Frenchman.

I never agreed with her. I'd had a love affair with France for as long as I could remember. Now, more than ever, I wholeheartedly disagreed with her. Sure, to the untrained eye most of the French seem to have two different moods: bored and downright disgusted.

Stereotypical.

After spending time in the library with Étienne, I'd learned one shouldn't judge a book by its cover. That's what I was thinking as I arrived at the center about half an hour later, a little more clearheaded than when I left Étienne, and beginning to feel the emotional fallout of our shameless library floor show.

Oh God. I remembered the annoyed expression on the librarian's face. Was it really *me* standing there with my shirt unbuttoned while a man caressed my breasts in public? Well, that was the beauty of being a stranger in a strange land. If that had happened in Orlando, I would've—well, never mind. It wouldn't have happened in Orlando. Blake *never* kissed me that passionately, even in the beginning of our relationship, even in the privacy of our dark bedroom. He was much too staid, much too dull.

Another cue that clueless me should have picked up on. My God, I was starting to form a list:

Five Clues My Husband Was Gay

1. He had better decorating sense than I did. Of course, I attributed it to the fact that he was an architect and worked with designers....

2. We could walk on the beach and his hair looked better at the end of the walk than when we started. Of course, Blake hated the beach—too messy, all that sand tracking up the car—so we didn't go much. The hair thing could have been a fluke....

3. He counted calories more stringently than my physically fit girlfriends. Okay, I never could justify that one....

4. His blatant lack of interest in sex—with me, anyway. Which leads me full circle—

5. Never in the eighteen-year span of our relationship did he kiss me as passionately as Étienne did today, not even in the beginning of our relationship. Blake was much too polite to fondle my breasts in public. Much too...gay.

Was it any wonder my body hummed at Étienne's touch? Yes, it *hummed*. Maybe I wasn't just drunk on the wine, I was drunk from being touched the way a woman should be touched.

Okay, actually, I *was* drunk from the wine, but my body *had* hummed.

My God, he wanted to be my lover. What was wrong with me? I guess the humming-body should negate the no-chemistry excuse. Shouldn't it?

I'd nearly failed chemistry in high school. So what did I know about it?

Maybe I was being hasty in writing him off. I mean, before I started analyzing the possibility of being his lover, my body responded. Maybe it wasn't a chemistry issue as much as I was just unprimed.

Maybe a younger lover was just what I needed to prime the old pump?

"Oh my God."

I sighed as I followed the path around a sharp, tree-lined bend and ran smack into Jacques Jauvert.

"Oh! *Bonjour,*" I said. Oh, yuck. It was the first time I'd seen the curmudgeon since the opening reception and—

He wasn't alone. Oooh…he was with one of the other residents—the guy from Argentina, I think—and they looked a little startled to see me.

"*Bonjour.*" Jauvert did not smile. The Argentinean stood stoically with his arms crossed. I got the distinct impression I'd *interrupted* something because they stood a little too close, even for the French. I'd bet money Jauvert wasn't dissing Mr. Argentina's artwork.

Ha, ha, ha, *ookay*, I got it. Ya didn't have to tell me

twice. My gaydar was fixed and fully operational. Hey, I'd just completed my Blake list, hadn't I?

Not a problem. Despite what happened with my husband, I didn't care what Jauvert's or Mr. Argentina's preferences were. Live and let live, that had always been my motto—just as long as Jauvert extended the same courtesy to my flowers.

The three yards I had to walk to pass them were the most awkward three yards I'd ever walked, but I rounded the next bend without another word and walked to my bungalow feeling a little woozy and a lot more uncertain about whether to make a midnight rendezvous with Étienne.

Come to me at midnight and I promise you won't regret it. The promise made my breath hitch.

The sculptor's studio door was open. I tuned in to read the emotional barometer. Were he and his lady fighting or making love? Though I'd never actually heard them doing the latter.

All was quiet and it hit me that it was a sad state when life came down to listening to see if I could hear other people making love.

Then I remembered Étienne.

I could make love if I wanted to.

The wind seemed to confirm as much. A strong gust blew through the courtyard, sounding the wind chimes above the sculptor's door.

The fat tomcat lay in a diminishing puddle of late-afternoon sunshine. His food dish was empty. He looked at me and *yowled*, a plaintive sound, as though he expected me to inform him when dinner would be served.

"What?" I said, unlocking my door.

He sauntered over and wound around my legs in that languid, sensual manner of a cat. I bent down and scratched him behind the ears.

"I'm sorry, I don't have anything for you."

He purred and nudged my hand into another stroke, walking away so my hand trailed the length of his back and tail. I noticed a tag on his collar read Guerrier. If I remembered correctly, *Guerrier* was French for *warrior*. He started to turn around for more, but a bird landed on the ground by the stucco studio wall and the cat lunged for it.

"I can't say I blame you, buddy. Don't wait for someone to serve you dinner. If you don't go get it yourself you just might miss out altogether."

The bird flew away and Guerrier plopped down as if the exertion had exhausted him.

As I stood to let myself inside I saw the sculptor at the window of his studio. He didn't wave or acknowledge me before he disappeared from view. I wondered if he even saw me.

At eleven forty-five that night, I exited the Odéon metro station and walked down the boulevard Saint Germain to the rue de l'Ancienne Comédie. The street was flooded with people and the city was just starting to come alive.

It only took me five minutes to make it to Étienne's *crêperie*. As I approached, I noticed a group of four beautiful young women, early twenties, standing at the counter talking to him.

I hung back and watched. Perhaps they were ordering. But there was something in the way Étienne stood leaning with his elbows on the counter talking to them, something in the way they flipped their hair and laughed at what he said to them. Although I couldn't hear what he said.

Whether it was their microminiskirts or the way they carried their firm young bodies, I, now perfectly sober after our drunken afternoon gropefest, suddenly found the chasm that spanned the twelve years between us insurmountable.

I shoved my purse—and the five condoms tucked in the inside pocket—up under my arm and went home.

It wasn't because I was jealous of the younger women—well, maybe I envied their youth. It was a strange feeling for me because I'd never had a problem with age. But I would have felt like his mother walking up to greet him in my sandals that I thought were strappy and sexy, but now seemed like sensible shoes next to the young Parisian women.

I must have been crazy—or drunk—coming out at this hour to meet him.

Up on the boulevard Saint Germain, I hailed a cab rather than braving the metro at midnight, and rode back to the center.

The lights were still on in the sculptor's studio. No music or sounds of conversation, only the smell of his cigarette mixing with the jasmine—his calling card.

I went inside feeling foolish about how I had spent the day. I knew I should just let it go, there was no harm in getting drunk and making out in a public place with a man who was so much younger—then I cringed and flung my purse onto the couch.

What was I doing here? Why had I even come?

I wanted to be home in my studio by the lake; I wanted to be in a place where people bought my flowers; I wanted to talk to Rita. I glanced at my watch. With the time difference, it wasn't even six-thirty in the morning. She'd kill me if I called her this early, especially if it was to tell her that I had the chance to have sex but turned it down.

I went into the kitchen to see if there was anything to eat and all I found was a wedge of cheese starting to grow mold, a few shriveled-looking strawberries, a hunk of stale baguette, some coffee and—*ugh*—more red wine.

As I dumped the wasted food in the garbage can, a sad feeling washed over me. It wasn't the young women or Étienne or the age difference that made me run away tonight.

It was me.

Pure and simple, it was *me*.

Would I ever be able to love or make love again without the dark shadow of doubt hanging in the back of my mind? That there was something fundamentally wrong with me looming in the back of my mind?

I started shaking as the feeling seeped into my bone marrow. I pressed my hands to my face and my mind whirled from Étienne to Blake to Jauvert.

"No! I am not going to stand here and implode."

I got the bed painting from the patio and put it on the easel. I splashed bold strokes of color onto the white sheets, intensified the angles and shadows on the sculptor's face, and for want of being able to capture the blonde's features, I painted him in bed with a woman who ended up looking remarkably like Camille Deveau. She was lying on her back with her head hanging slightly over the edge of the wildly colored bed. The sculptor, with his wide, naked shoulders, lush mouth and seductive eyes was on top of her in the full throes of coital ecstasy.

I painted until the sun rose, throwing onto the canvas all the pent-up frustration I harbored over not being able to go to Étienne; all the hurt over Blake's lies; and all the anger for all those wasted years I stayed with a man who didn't love me the way I deserved to be loved.

CHAPTER 10

I awoke the next day to the sound of loud voices. Before I could force open my eyes, it sounded as if they were fighting right over me.

Oh, for God's sake. This was getting old.

I sat up and rubbed my eyes with my paint-splotched hands. I picked at the color that was caked under my fingernails.

The noise had faded and I wondered for a moment if I'd dreamt it. So I got up and kneaded my stiff neck as I looked at my watch.

It was one o'clock in the afternoon. A rush of guilt flooded through me. Staying up all night and sleeping away the day was becoming a habit.

I hadn't partied the night away or whiled away the hours making love….

I'd spent a drunken afternoon that almost led me to such exploits. I cringed as I thought about last night's close call with Étienne, and amazingly enough, rather than beating myself up over it, I was relieved nothing happened. My feelings confirmed that while I liked Étienne, I was right in not taking him as my lover.

I studied the canvas I'd worked on so hard all night. See, I'd gotten something done last night. No need to beat myself up over the turned-around days and nights.

I stared at the image, at the bright, wild colors and the way I'd defined the sculptor's face. Wow, it really did look like him. And I wasn't even a portrait painter. Not bad, if I did say so myself.

Now, the image of him making love to Camille Deveau... Hmm, I'd have to think about that. Perhaps I needed to paint over it and start again?

I decided to deliberate in the shower.

After I'd dressed in jeans and a short-sleeved mock turtleneck, leaving my hair down to air dry, I realized I was so hungry I considered eating the canvas rather than painting over Madame Deveau. So I grabbed my purse, not bothering to take the condoms out of the inner pocket, and stepped out of the studio to go to the market.

I had just shut and locked my door when the blonde came flying out of the sculptor's studio, shrieking at the top of her lungs, tears making her mascara run down her face in grotesque black streaks.

The sculptor was not far behind her.

"Matilde!"

He yelled something else after her. She stopped at the head of the path that led away from our courtyard and he caught up with her. He placed his hands on her shoulders and shook her gently, but she just cried and allowed herself to be shaken, like a rag doll in the hands of a child. Until she fell against him and sobbed, muttering something that sounded like a plea for—forgiveness? For love?

What? I wished I understood what they were saying.

Especially when he shook his head and repeated, "*Non.*" Over and over, to everything she said, which just made her cry harder.

Was he breaking up with her?

It seemed so when she threw her arms around his neck and tried to kiss him, but he pushed her away.

"*Non!*" More unintelligible French. More hysterical sobs from the blonde.

Oh my God, is he gay, too?

Was the entire male population gay and I just didn't realize it?

Well, no, Étienne wasn't, but ugh, that was another problem unto itself.

Why else would the sculptor reject such a stunning woman who was so obviously in love with him?

He held her and let her sob into his chest for a few minutes and then he put a protective arm around her and they walked off together. He murmured soft French to her as they disappeared around the bend.

Well, now I knew what it felt like to be invisible, which was probably a good thing because it would have been very embarrassing if they'd realized I'd been watching them.

When I got to the gate, I saw that they'd turned to the left and were walking on the sidewalk. To avoid being seen, I kept a fair distance behind them. But I was so curious to know where they were going. Were they breaking up or was this just another chapter in their volatile relationship?

If I followed them I'd be able to observe the blonde and I might be able to paint her likeness over Camille's face in *The Bed*. I'd have to paint in the mascara streaks. Even though it seemed a little extreme, it went well with the dramatic feel of the painting.

I followed them for miles, across the River Seine, from the left bank to the right, until they turned onto rue Pigalle. Not the nicest part of Paris. Even the air smelled different here—vaguely of garbage and cigar smoke melded with the cloying perfume and the sweat of broken dreams.

During World War Two, American servicemen called this district "Pig Alley," because of all the hookers, sordid strip joints and sleazy sex clubs.

Although, I'd heard that it was starting to become a mecca for the famous creative types, at face value, it looked as if not much had changed.

I strolled past Joy's Sex Emporium and a place called Le Star Dust—Sexy Follies. The front of Le Star Dust was painted purple and a graffiti-covered metal security door was pulled halfway down over the entrance.

Right next door was what looked like a pawnshop. The sign hanging out over the sidewalk read Change, but the *g* was broken on the sign over the doorway and it read, Chance.

Which was it? Change or chance?

Perhaps one facilitated the other?

The sculptor and the blonde stopped in the middle of the sidewalk. She broke down in another fit, hitting him, banging on his chest with her fists, slapping him in the face before she ran away—in my direction.

To avoid being seen, I doubled back a few storefronts to a café, where I waited for them to pass.

When I emerged, I didn't see them in either direction. Either they'd ducked into a shop—a sex shop?— or they'd been swallowed up by the curious Pigalle crowds.

I walked up to rue Fontaine, wondering if perchance they'd somehow gotten back by me when I turned into the café. They weren't there.

Just as well. What was I supposed to do if I found them? Tell them I'd followed them to study the blonde's face for my painting? Or that I was dying to know what on earth they'd been fighting about over the three weeks I'd been here? Or perhaps I could explain that since coming to Paris, I'd been prone to flights of fancy that more often than not turned out to be wild-goose chases?

I sighed, seeing the most truth in the last claim.

But I could always keep this from becoming a flight of fancy if I had a look around.

That's what I did, for a long time. As the hours gave way one into the other, I wandered the streets, absorbing the strange and exotic sights of Paris's red-light district.

The lurid neon signs of the Sexodrome and the Musée de l'Érotisme were muted by the golden glow of the late-afternoon sun. Scantily clad prostitutes sprawled in brightly painted doorways lining the rue Fontaine. Most of them called out to me. Obviously, anyone who was willing to pay for services was welcome.

Women, some of whom I guessed were transvestites, hailed taxis on the rue Pigalle. Were they on their way to work the Bois de Boulogne on the west side?

Jauvert's introductory letter advised us to avoid the Bois at night. No matter how beautiful and serene the park seemed by day, he said, it transformed into the sleazy underbelly of the city after sunset. Perhaps, here before me in living color, were its inhabitants.

I wandered, mesmerized and sickened by the darker side of the City of Light; drawn in by this quarter where scandalous luxury mated with utter wretchedness in a streetside freak show that lured one closer, closer to the flame, until, I imagined, it consumed body and soul. Why had the sculptor and the blonde come here? Did one of them live here? Did they come here to indulge some kinky fetish? Maybe that's what had the blonde so riled up.

I strolled in awe through the curious blend of exquisite landmarks, such as the Moulin Rouge, and old burlesque theaters. I marveled at how the sex shops and prostitutes mixed with the occasional bourgeois building and the hordes of tourists.

It was all there: hope and despair, opportunity seeker and opportunist, wide-eyed innocent and jaded exhibitionist—stewing and melding, the stench lingering in the fetid air.

Did dreams beckon these people to Paris? Or had they, too, run away from the past? Selling their souls for a few months' reprieve or a way to anesthetize themselves against the future?

As the initial voyeuristic curiosity subsided, I decided Pigalle, simultaneously cruel and cunning, was no different from any other place in the world. The lost souls I'd seen wandering the street were not so dissimilar from me.

At least my running away from life in Orlando had plucked me from a soul-snuffing existence and deposited me into a situation ripe with opportunity for growth.

I guess it really was all up to me whether I grew or spent three months spinning my wheels.

As the sun set over Paris's eighteenth arrondissement, I decided it *was* up to me whether my Paris would be cruel or kind. But before I could decide, first I had to find my way back home.

I decided to take the metro since I was hungry and tired after walking around all day. I dug through my purse to get my train pass out of my wallet and discovered my wallet was missing.

Oh, for God's sake, did someone lift it out of my purse as I wandered the streets like a wide-eyed tourist? I turned in a quick circle as if I'd see someone standing close by looking through it.

People rushed past me in a hurry to get on the metro, but no one had my wallet. I checked the bottom of my purse to see if any coins had fallen out, but no luck. I even contemplated trying to push my way through on the tail of paying riders, but this was a station with large sliding doors that opened and shut fast and hard, allowing just one person to make it through.

If worst came to worst, perhaps I could find another metro station with turnstile entrances. And risk the chance of being caught?

I thought about the signs: Chance. Change. My legs ached as I mounted the steps to take me back up to the street.

I went to the closest café to ask for directions to the next closest metro station. The place wasn't as crowded as I thought it would be based on the steady flow of traffic outside.

I walked up to the bar.

"Excusez-moi, s'il vous plaît." The bartender cocked a brow at me and I said, *"Parlez-vous anglais?"*

Please speak English.

"Non." His voice was gruff, but he held up a finger, which I guessed meant he wanted me to wait. So I did, and that's when I noticed the sculptor seated across the

bar in all his dark, rough-hewn glory. The blonde was not with him.

He must have sensed someone watching because he glanced up, but I ducked my head so he wouldn't catch me staring.

The bartender came back and said something in French to no one in particular.

"I speak English," said my neighbor.

The bartender gestured to me. I felt completely transparent, as if the sculptor knew I'd followed him up here. But then I decided it was a ridiculous thought. How could he know?

"May I help you?" he said from across the bar.

"I'm looking for the closest metro station. Um, beyond the one out there."

He nodded, downed his espresso, shoved his Gitane cigarettes in his pocket and tossed a few bills on the bar.

"I will show you."

"Oh, thank you, but that's not necessary. If you'll just point me in the right direction I can manage."

He ran a hand over the whiskered shadow on his cheeks and said, "A pretty foreigner should not wander the streets of Pigalle alone at night—unless she is seeking *that* sort of thing."

That sort of thing?

Pretty foreigner?—Ha, there's that word again—*pretty*. Just like…*pretty*, decorative little florals.

"I am on my way home." He walked around the bar and stood in front of me. I hadn't realized just how tall and broad-shouldered he was. "You might as well come with me." My heart nearly leaped out of my chest. Oh my God, he *did* know. Or…wait…perhaps he thought I was after *that sort of thing*.

"I don't know you, *monsieur*. Why would I go with you?"

He laughed, and if I hadn't been so nervous, I might have liked the way his eyes crinkled at the corners in George Clooney fashion.

"Don't play coy. I am Jean Luc Le Garric. We are neighbors. You followed me up here this afternoon, *non?*"

CHAPTER 11

Maybe it was the fallout of seeing so many transvestites and prostitutes in one place, and all those hungry eyes and greedy hands eager to devour half-naked bodies and strip souls bare, but I was glad to get out of Pigalle.

I was glad to have someone accompany me home.

Even though I was embarrassed that Jean Luc Le Garric knew I'd followed him and even though I had to swallow my pride and borrow metro fare from him, my feet hurt so badly and I was so hungry that it was worth it.

Outside the café, he paused. "I don't understand why you want a different metro station. This is the one that will best take you home."

I couldn't bring myself to tell him I needed a station with turnstiles rather than doors so I could scoot through without paying. He'd think I was a complete and utter freak. If he didn't already.

So, I did the only thing I could do: I played dumb.

"Oh, I didn't realize that. Well, I guess you saved me a lot of needless walking."

Once we were on the train, he sat next to me. His long legs in their dark jeans bumped the seat in front of us. "Let me see your metro map. I will show you how to read it. To save you needless walking."

My cheeks flushed hot and I couldn't look at him. "I don't have it with me."

"You do not know Paris and yet you go out without a map and without your wallet? Is this how you do things in America?"

"My wallet may have been stolen."

"Did you report it to the police?"

"No. It might be in my studio. Last night, after I got home, I tossed my purse on the couch and it might have fallen out. At least that's what I'm hoping."

"Well if you insist on being a *flâneuse* at least make sure you have your map with you."

I blinked. "A what?"

"A *flâneuse*." I liked the way his accent caused the last syllables of the word to do an upturn, even though I had no idea what he was talking about.

He must have gathered as much because he said, "A *flâneur* is one who wanders the streets. Many great artists were notorious *flâneurs*. A *flâneuse* is a female wanderer."

A wanderer. I liked that.

The train stopped. A man in our car got out and a mother and her two children boarded.

"Does your girlfriend live in Pigalle?"

"My girlfriend? I do not have a girlfriend."

Oh. Perhaps they did break up.

"The woman who comes to your studio every day. I hear you arguing. Lucky for you my French is so poor. I don't mean to be nosy, but she's very beautiful and she seems to be crazy about you. Are you sure there's no way to work it out?"

He squinted at me, dark brown eyes that slanted down at the corners, framed by long, black lashes. "Do you speak of Matilde?"

"Is that her name?"

"Matilde is not my lover. Though she would like to be. That is why we fight. She is only my model, or she used to be. Her work with me is finished."

He was a bit arrogant.

"Matilde, hmm?" How could a heterosexual man refuse to be her lover? "She is so beautiful."

He made a disgusted noise designed to end the conversation and stared straight ahead as the train hummed along. I think it was the first time I'd ever ridden the metro when a busker wasn't in my face with his music. What I wouldn't give for the strains of an accordion or an off-key singer belting out, "I love Paris in the springtime…" That way I wouldn't feel such a competing need to fill the silence.

"So, I gather you are not part of the exchange program?"

"*Non.* I am a native Parisian."

"Really? I was under the impression that the

Delacroix Centre was strictly an exchange center. Are you the only permanent artist?"

"*Oui.*"

"I would love to see your work sometime."

He nodded.

He didn't say anything else such as, *Sure, come on over,* or *How about when we get home?* I took the hint from his short answers that I should quit asking questions. I mean, after all, he was nice enough to help me out of a bind. If not for him, I would still be walking.

We traveled in silence, changing trains twice, until we finally arrived at the École Militaire stop. It was beginning to feel familiar.

"This is us." He stood back and let me exit the train ahead of him. When we popped up onto the street again, night had fallen on the city and the air had taken on a chill. I ran my hands over my arms trying to warm up. As a native Floridian, I still wasn't in the habit of grabbing a jacket when I went out.

"You are cold?" Jean Luc asked.

I nodded.

"Please, take my jacket."

He placed it on my shoulders, the bulk of it hanging large on my frame. It smelled of cigarettes, cologne and man. The gesture touched me. It made me think of how gently he'd placed his arm around Matilde and how she'd leaned into him. Who could blame her for feeling the way she did?

I wished I could talk to her and tell her I knew how it

felt to love a man who was emotionally unavailable. And that she would be… She would be okay. Eventually.

"How do you like Paris?" Jean Luc's voice startled me out of my thoughts.

"I like it. It has so much to offer. I really feel as if I'm just getting my bearings. And one third of the residency is over."

We turned down the pedestrian market street, rue Cler. All the shops were closed up for the night and it reminded me I had no food in the kitchen. Delicious aromas wafted from the café at the corner of rue Bosquet—people dined on sumptuous-looking meals that made my stomach growl. I put my hand over my belly and glanced up at Jean Luc.

He smiled. "Are you hungry?"

I nodded. "I set out to the market this afternoon, but somehow I ended up in Pigalle instead."

Shaking his head, he stopped in front of the café.

"Why don't we get something to eat."

"Oh, I would love to, but I don't have my wallet. Remember?"

"I am inviting you to be my guest."

A woman passed by with a tray loaded with bread, a carafe of white wine, some sort of chicken dish and a salad niçoise, the green beans, boiled eggs, potatoes and olives artfully arranged on the plate.

My mouth watered just looking at it.

"I should be taking you out to dinner for rescuing me."

He walked on ahead and I followed him. "We shall

go see my friend Michel at the Bistro du Mars. It is just around the corner. Have you been there?"

I'd passed by this restaurant many times on my way home from shopping on the rue Cler but had never stopped and eaten there. In Paris there were so many restaurants it was almost overwhelming.

We stepped inside the intimate space that was no larger than my living room at home and had seating for about ten parties. Two of the tables were occupied, one with a couple and the other with a family of three.

Delectable smells greeted us and the white lace curtains and starched tablecloths stood out brilliantly against the red velvet banquettes, red carpet and textured red wallpaper.

"Jean Luc!" A tall, thin woman who looked to be in her midfifties, with a straight black chin-length bob moved gracefully from behind the bar toward us. She removed her rimless, rectangular glasses, which she wore low on her nose, before kissing him on each cheek and bubbling over in exuberant French. From the few words I understood, I gathered it had been a while since he'd been in.

"Marie-Grace, please allow me to introduce my friend and neighbor—" Jean Luc looked at me blankly and I realized I'd never told him my name.

"*Enchantée, madame. Je m'appelle* Annabelle."

"She is an American in Paris for the exchange program at the Delacroix Centre."

"Ahh, *enchantée, madame*." Marie-Grace shoved her glasses back on, gave me the once-over, then leaned in and air-kissed both of my cheeks.

In the very back of the restaurant, a man in a white chef's coat opened a little window, set out two plates of salad and called a hearty greeting.

"Please, be seated." Marie-Grace gestured to a table in the corner. Then she and Jean Luc walked to the window. Marie-Grace retrieved the food and Jean Luc and the man, whom I presumed to be Michel, talked for a few minutes.

When I sat down, I realized how thoroughly exhausted I was. Starved and bone tired, but not too tired to watch Jean Luc at the back of the restaurant.

I decided his longish, curly dark hair made him look kind of like the actor Olivier Martinez. Olivier Martinez with amazing full lips, mile-wide shoulders and George Clooney eyes.

Lord, the combination worked.

Marie-Grace set a basket of fresh French bread and a carafe of water on the table, humming as she worked. It was a nice content sound and I relaxed into the red velvet banquette and watched Jean Luc walk toward me.

He ordered a bottle of white burgundy and we both took Marie-Grace's recommendation for the Dover sole.

When she walked away to place our order, Jean Luc said, "So, Annabelle, I may call you Annabelle, *non?*"

I nodded.

"Will you please explain why you were following me today?"

* * *

Thank God for good service.

Marie-Grace brought the wine just as I started to panic.

I managed to stammer out, "Well, it's complicated."

Voilà, she appeared with the bottle.

"Won't you have a drink with us?" I had no idea whether inviting the restaurateur to join you for a drink violated some esoteric French custom. All I knew was that it bought me more time.

"How lovely of you to ask, but I must decline so I may tend to my patrons." She nodded and resumed her humming as she walked away.

"That was a nice try," said Jean Luc. "But even if she would have joined us, I would not have forgotten the question, which was, will you please explain why you were following me today?"

I sipped my wine and tried to avoid looking at his eyes, but I could feel his penetrating gaze watching me, waiting expectantly.

I set down my glass and took a deep breath. "I don't know why I followed you. Are you in some kind of trouble where you'd have to worry about being tailed?"

He laughed, and I was glad because it lightened the mood.

"No, I'm not in any sort of trouble. That's why I get alarmed when I discover someone is watching my every move."

"If someone did not know the circumstance, that could sound very paranoid."

"I suppose it might." He lifted the cloth on the bread-basket and offered me some. I took a piece and put it on my bread plate, ignoring my rumbling tummy, waiting to see where this conversation was leading before I tore into the food.

I folded my hands in my lap and leaned in. "Okay, here's the truth." Or at least part of the truth. "I've listened to you and your...Matilde fighting almost daily since I arrived. You're very loud, did you know that?"

He shook his head. "I was not aware. I beg your pardon."

He picked up some bread, tore off a piece and spread it with butter. "And you were saying?"

I watched his sexy full lips as he bit into the bread.

"I was just curious about you. That's all." I sipped my wine. Over the top of my glass, I watched as his throat worked in a swallow.

"So what you are confessing is that you are nosy."

I almost choked. "I'm not nosy. I'm just..."

He smiled. His eyes crinkled and I lost my train of thought. My mind jumped back to the night I saw him standing in the window wearing the red bandanna, and my stomach fluttered. This time it wasn't because of hunger.

"You are poking fun at me," I said.

The image of him in the red bandanna made me remember Matilde standing naked in his studio and how he swore they were never lovers. He *had to be* gay to not want her.

I was such an idiot. After what I'd been through with Blake was I *really* developing a crush on a gay man? There was probably some sad psychological disorder that made women go after unattainable men.

His brows knit. "Poking fun? I do not understand."

Damn language barrier. I twisted the napkin in my lap. "Making fun of me?"

He stared at me blankly.

"Come on, your English is very good, surely you understand what I'm saying."

He arched a brow. "I am having fun at your expense."

I blinked once. Twice.

"Okay, you're a joker, aren't you? You knew exactly what I was saying." I buttered my bread and bit into it.

"Well, then, since I have a good sense of humor, I suppose I shall forgive you for following me today."

There was something in his gaze, the way it lingered bold and assessing, slowly and seductively searching my face, lingering on my lips, before returning to my eyes.

My head swam and my heart turned over.

Okay, maybe I'd been hasty. Gay men did not look at women the way he was looking at me.

We spent the rest of the evening talking about wine, the best nontouristy places to go in Paris, art—I learned that he taught sculpting at the École des Beaux-Arts, Paris's prestigious art school, a job he relished because he could divide his time between the school and his studio—and my new-found theories about Camille Deveau and Georges Fonteneau's secret relationship. Yes, he'd heard of her, but not their purported love affair.

"It's such a sad story. Loving a man she can't have. I can relate to this woman on so many levels."

"Did you come to Paris to escape a love you could not have?"

I stared at the candle through the golden pool of wine in my glass.

"I'll make a deal with you—tell me why you don't want to be Matilde's lover, how you could refuse such a beautiful woman who is obviously crazy about you, and I'll explain exactly how I relate to Camille Deveau and why I came to Paris. See, you'll get a two-for-one."

He dipped his head in acceptance. "Touché." He touched his glass to mine. "The situation with Matilde is complicated. But just in case you wondered, I did not reject her because I do not like women. *Au contraire*. I like women very much."

Oh.

Something flared inside me so intense it made my breath catch in my chest. I'd never felt so comfortable so fast with a man. He was funny and interesting, not to mention what he did to me when he smiled.

On the way home, walking on the uneven sidewalk under an indigo sky so starry it could have been a Van Gogh painting, I said, "So you knew I was your neighbor? I always thought you weren't aware of me."

"Unaware? Of you? *Non*. I saw you peering through your windows at me."

I swatted him on the arm, noting that even earlier today, I would have been mortified to know he saw me watching him. But now I was completely at ease. "How come you didn't wave or say hello?"

"Are you kidding? Every time I would look out at you, you would turn your head or rush away from the window. I thought you were very unfriendly."

I laughed. If you only knew.

He waited with me as I unlocked the door. I realized, as I slid the key in the lock, I didn't want the evening to end.

On a wild hair, I said, "Would you like to come in? I have a bottle of red I've been needing a good excuse to open. Perhaps you'll accept a glass of wine in lieu of me reimbursing you for the metro ticket?"

"I think that sounds like an equitable exchange." He followed me inside.

"Make yourself at home." I went into the kitchen, opened the wine and got two glasses.

When I came back into the living room, he was standing in front of my easel…looking at *The Bed* painting.

CHAPTER 12

Jean Luc arched a brow seductively. He tilted his head to the left and stared at the canvas.

"I recognize the man. It's an excellent likeness of me. But I must know, who is the beautiful woman I'm...*with?*" I set the wineglasses on the coffee table, trying to figure out how to explain why I'd painted such an intimate portrait of him. When I straightened, his gorgeous eyes were watching me, looking smug and amazed, as if he'd caught me naked. But the French didn't have nudity hang-ups. Americans had cornered that market, and in true form, I felt naked and exposed standing there unable to explain it away.

For a few breathless seconds, it felt as if my heart had stopped, until it kicked in and pounded double time and all the blood in my body rushed to my face.

"She's nobody," I said.

A reflex made me step forward and try to yank the painting off the easel. I just wanted to stash it out of sight, but Jean Luc stopped me with a firm, steady hand on top of mine. If I could've crawled under the couch I would have, but I couldn't even move my hand out from under his.

"*Personne?* Er, nobody?" His brows knit and he moved in closer to study the image of the woman. "She looks like your painter Deveau, the one with whom you identify. No?" A sly, knowing smile spread across his face.

"No." I jerked my hand away, and followed his gaze to the Camille Deveau biography lying on the table next to my easel.

Oh, God.

He picked it up, studying the photograph of her on the cover and looked back at the canvas. "You really are an accomplished portrait artist. I am impressed. And flattered."

I opened my mouth to say something, anything, racking my brain for a way out of this mortifying mess, but all that came out in one breathless rush was the truth.

"I intended to paint you with Matilde, but I never could capture her features." I turned around and walked back to the coffee table. With my back to him, I picked up my glass and gulped the wine. "Somehow Camille Deveau crept into your bed."

"And you see yourself in this tragic French painter? Is that why you painted her in my bed?"

I shrugged, still turned away from him.

"Does that mean you fancy yourself in my bed?"

My mind whirled and I heard his footsteps on the wooden floor. He stopped behind me.

Placing his hands on my shoulders, he gently turned me around and lifted my chin until I looked at him.

His question hung in the air between us as palpable

as a lover's kiss, and he traced my bottom lip with his knuckle.

My body ached for his touch, and I caught his finger gently between my teeth, closing my eyes as I closed my lips around it.

"Come here," he murmured.

I don't know who moved first, but the next thing I knew we were in each other's arms.

His kiss sent new spirals of ecstasy unfurling in my body. I couldn't remember when I'd wanted a man as much as I wanted him.

I didn't care about Matilde or Blake or that Jean Luc had seen the painting. All I knew was, yes, I was the woman who should be in his bed.

I didn't end up in his bed.

He ended up in mine.

Thank God for Rita's going-away gift. Three down. Ninety-seven to go. It was a beautiful night.

He left at four-thirty because he had an early class to teach. I offered to get up and fix him some coffee, but he just kissed me and said, "Stay in bed. I'll see you later this afternoon."

I couldn't sleep after he left. I tossed and turned, the scent of our love still in the air. The day's turn of events swam in my head, merging with the Pigalle freak show.

I turned over and lay on my back, stretching my naked body. This time yesterday I never dreamt Jean Luc Le Garric would be in my bed.

This time yesterday I didn't even know his name was Jean Luc. He was simply the sculptor across the way. My, my, how fast things changed.

I got up, pulled on my big white shirt and padded into the kitchen on bare feet to fix myself a pot of coffee. As it brewed, I saw the corner of my wallet sticking out from beneath a pillow on the old couch. It must have fallen out of my purse when I tossed the bag on the sofa after my wild goose chase to see Étienne. Finding it was a good omen. Yes, a very good sign.

With a hot cup in my hand, I put a blank canvas on my easel and drew with paint the image of one of the prostitutes I'd seen draped over a cobalt-painted chair in the bright red doorway of a sex shop.

A painted lady on a painted chair in a painted doorway.

It worked. I would call it simply *The Painted Lady*. The scene came from a new place in me just recently awakened. Albeit the image wasn't pretty, but there would be no more "…*pretty*, decorative little florals…."

At least not while I was in Paris.

Strange though, until now, I'd never aspired to the kind of painting that archived life. Life happened all around me. I always thought it was the egotistical souls who fancied their lives so interesting they were compelled to immortalize it on canvas.

That's why I painted flowers.

Maybe I painted flowers because nothing else around me was interesting enough to paint? Until now.

Obviously.

I sighed and drew brown streaks through the prostitute's blond hair. The thought of abandoning my flowers didn't settle well. I felt like a traitor, as if I was abandoning who I really was rather than growing into something bigger.

I stepped back and considered my work, then painted a crown of daisies on the hooker's head and a basket of roses at her feet.

I worked fast, using quick, shorthand strokes to rough in the images in my mind before the vivid details faded: the way a transvestite's miniskirt hiked up in back as he got into a cab, the tattooed woman in the sequined thong and itty-bitty bikini top that exposed half moons of dark nipples as she danced under the Folies Pigalle sign, the lingerie-clad "hostess" asleep in the window of the cabaret…

At about ten o'clock, when my stomach demanded I go to the market to pick up some breakfast, I was just wiping my paint-stained hands on a rag when someone knocked on the door. Contemplating not answering since I wasn't dressed, I peeked out a louver in the shutters to see who it was.

My breath caught. Jean Luc.

I was a mess. I wasn't expecting him for hours. Even so, I wasn't about to leave him standing out there.

I opened the door and he smiled that smile that made me dizzy, holding a loaf of bread, some cheese, salami and the most beautiful bouquet of mixed spring flowers.

"You weren't supposed to be here until this afternoon." I leaned in and kissed him long and deep. "I haven't even showered or dressed."

He didn't say a word, but dropped the groceries and flowers and pulled me into his arms, sliding his hands under my shirt to cup my bare bottom and pull me into him.

In the foggy recesses of my memory I vaguely remembered a time when I would have been mortified at the thought of having a man touch me in such intimate places when I wasn't shower fresh... But that was another life.

Letting everything lie where it fell, Jean Luc scooped me up and carried me into the bedroom and we picked up where we left off early that morning.

Afterward, we lay in bed, my head on his shoulder, tucked into the crook of his neck. He held me possessively against him, gently stroking my arm.

"Ah, I forgot. The reason I came over here was to bring you a map. It would be a tragedy if my little *flâneuse* set out to wander and I was not there to help her find her way home."

I smiled up at him. "There's that word again. *Flâneuse*."

"You act as if it is something distasteful. But it is not. The French writer Baudelaire— You have heard of him, *non?*"

I nodded.

"He once wrote, 'For the perfect *flâneur*, it is an immense joy to set up house in the heart of the multitude, amid the ebb and flow. To be away from home, yet to feel oneself everywhere at home, to see the world, to be at the center of the world, yet to remain hidden from the world—such are a few of the slightest pleasures of those independent, passionate, impartial natures which the tongue can but clumsily define.'"

"That's incredible. Do you always go around quoting literature?"

He tucked his hands behind his head, looking smug and pleased with himself.

I breathed in his scent, a mix of green, tobacco, spice and sex. It smelled like heaven. I closed my eyes and buried my nose in his neck, certain that any minute I would awaken to learn the past twenty-four hours had been one sexy dream.

Please, just five more minutes…

I propped myself up on my elbow and looked at him. "You know, we've made love four times, and I haven't even seen your studio. When do I get the grand tour?"

"Whenever you'd like."

"I'm going to shower, since that's where I was heading when you appeared. Make no mistake—I am not complaining, but I do need to freshen up."

I wrapped a towel around myself and walked into the living room, blotting the excess water from my hair. "Jean Luc, what book was that Baudelaire piece you quoted—" Jean Luc stood at the door wearing nothing but his boxer shorts talking to Étienne.

Oh, shit.

While Jean Luc went out to get us something to eat, I called Rita.

"Oh my God. You had sex," said Rita. "I guess you're not homesick anymore?"

"Nope. All cured. He is incredible."

I fell back into the bed pillows and turned over on my side so I could sniff the pillowcase to see if it still smelled like him.

"Wait," said Rita. "Let me pour myself a glass of wine. Then I want details."

"Okay, hurry, he's going to be back soon and this is costing both of us a fortune." The line crackled as she set down the phone, but really I didn't care if it cost ten dollars a minute.

"I'm ready. Remember, details. Sexy details." I told her about Étienne and the library; about how I went to the restaurant at midnight but I couldn't go through with it and how he showed up at the door after Jean Luc and I had just had wild, passionate sex; and how Étienne was furious with me because I'd told him I didn't feel right about having sex because I was still married.

"Oh, you are such a liar."

"Well it was better than saying, 'Sorry, I'm just not that into you.'"

"Poor Étienne. It sounds like you broke his tender little heart."

"Something tells me Étienne's poor, tender little heart will be just fine. He'll find his middle-aged American woman to marry, he'll get his green card. He'll be happy, the woman will be *ecstatic* and they'll live happily ever after."

"Then get to the good stuff. So this other guy, Jean Luc? Is that his name?" She said it with a pinched, put-on French accent so it sounded more like Jaaahhn-Loook.

"Yes, that would be him." I flung my arm over my eyes and lay there smiling at the mental picture of him in my bed. "God, Ri, he's incredible."

"The sex is that good?"

"Mmm, hmm."

"Let me live vicariously through you. Details…"

"Which time?"

"Okay, nobody likes a braggart. But I'll forgive you and let you tell me about the steamiest, hottest, sexiest parts."

"All I'll say is that I haven't had this much fun since—I don't think I've ever had this much fun."

"So tell me…is he huge?"

"Ri! I can't believe you asked me that."

"Condom count? You are using them, aren't you?"

"Of course I am."

"How many?"

"Four."

"Four times? In twenty-four hours. I am so jealous. That's a good month for me. What about the blonde?"

I laughed to cover my annoyance.

"What about her? He said they're not involved."

"Yeah, right. Don't be naive."

"She was his model but not his lover. Did I tell you Ben's coming for a visit next month after his exams?"

"Anna! Don't change the subject and don't tell me you believe that line of crap about their being just friends. I saw them together. You don't fight like that unless you're doing it."

"Gee, thanks, Ri. Let's see if I have any other hot news you can pour ice water on."

I stared at the ceiling and willed myself not to succumb to the doubt.

"Rita, something's happened to me. It's like I'm finally free of all the shit that Blake put me through, and I'm talking eighteen years' worth. I look back now and I realize I never really lived. Until now."

Rita didn't respond.

"Everything's changed. My art's changed. I've changed. My God, I'm having red-hot, no-strings-attached sex—and might I add, it's the best sex I've ever had in my life. I'm happy, Rita, so don't spoil it."

I heard the front door open, the sound of Jean Luc rustling about in the kitchen. For a split second I wondered if going to the market was the only errand he ran. But I blinked away the thought as soon as it skittered into my head.

My sister sighed into the receiver. "I'm sorry. I am

happy you're happy. And I'm jealous as hell you're having red-hot sex. Even if you won't tell me about it."

"Is everything all right with you and Fred?"

"Oh, yeah. We're just…married." She chuckled and
the sound was kind of thin.

"Give him a hug for me, okay?"

I walked into the kitchen and mouthed the words *my
sister*. Jean Luc smiled at me. He walked over, picked up
my hair and started planting little kisses on the back of
my neck.

"I will," she said. "And, Anna, I really am happy for
you. That's why I left you the condoms, I wanted you
to have a good time while you were there. A *lot* of good
times. Just don't think you have to fall in love with the
first guy you sleep with. I don't want you to get hurt
again."

CHAPTER 13

One month later, lingering over cappuccinos with Jean Luc after a long walk through Luxembourg Gardens, it hit me. I had officially succumbed to the spell of springtime Paris. As we sat in companionable silence drinking in the city's charm, I couldn't remember the last time the chiding voices in my head were this quiet.

Here, in the heart of Paris, the voices quietly hummed a melodious tune, something vaguely familiar, but I couldn't quite put my finger on it.

Notes of promise?

I tilted my cup so that the dark coffee splashed up over the stiff white foam. It had been so long since I'd heard that tune, I couldn't remember. All I knew was it felt right.

Jean Luc lit a cigarette and turned his head to blow the smoke away from me.

"Will you to come to dinner with me at my parents' home on Sunday?"

Parents?

Over the month we'd been together he'd revealed a lot about himself—that he was forty-three years old, divorced for eight years and the father of a twenty-one-year-old daughter who went to college in Spain, which is where her mother lived.

When he wasn't at work or in his studio (where I now spent almost as much time as I did in my own), he was at his third-floor walk-up in a nineteenth-century building on the rue Guichard in the ritzy sixteenth arrondissement (teaching art in Paris must pay); his bedroom had an incredible, downy-soft featherbed, in which I could spend days (and we did when time permitted); his favorite kind of music was Portuguese fado; his favorite singer, Amália Rodriguez, owner of the sad, haunting voice I'd heard wailing from his studio before I met him; May was his favorite month of the year because the weather warmed up and he could enjoy the outdoors.

"En mai, fais ce qu'il te plaît." He said it meant, "In May, do what pleases you."

I loved the sound of that.

He told me he preferred to work all night and sleep all day, just like I did, but he said it was tough to pull it off when he had to teach an early class, and that he'd fallen into the upside-down cycle because he did not have anyone to share his bed at night.

I thought of all the times I'd heard Matilde and him laughing and fighting in the wee hours. And even worse, all the times when I saw the light on in his studio but I didn't hear them. But I hadn't seen hide nor hair of Matilde since that day I followed them to Pigalle. The day everything began.

I refused to let my mind create monsters because things were good. Too good. Not too-good-to-be-true. Just too good to mar with doubt over the shadow of a young, beautiful woman who was once a part of his life but seemed to have all but vanished.

I tried to ask about her, but he still refused to talk about her. Even after I spilled my guts over the reason my eighteen-year marriage ended.

I was starved for information about him, for clues to what composed the heart and soul of this complex, sexy man who was slowly but surely sweeping me off my feet.

One day when I went to an Internet café to do more research on Camille Deveau, I ended up typing in *Jean Luc Le Garric* instead. Here, I learned about his critically acclaimed Munich exhibit last March; it happened around the time I found out about Blake. How strange to put events that happened in his life before we met into context with mine.

Via the Internet, I also discovered he'd served on the faculty of the École des Beaux-Arts for fifteen years and was among the elite who'd graduated from said prestigious art school with unanimous accolades from his final-examination jury. A feat rarely accomplished by the few who gain admission to the school.

I knew all this, yet I hadn't heard a single word about his parents. I didn't even realize they lived locally.

Until now.

Family. That was so normal.

I was a woman who loved the calm comfort of family. The excitement of romance was fun for a while, but what I really craved was the simple security of family, the safety of it, the simplicity of it, the way you could come home and kick off your shoes, change into your jammies early on a Friday night and curl up on the couch.

In the days preceding the dinner, I felt alternately giddy and paralyzed at the prospect of dining with his family.

Because it was *his* family. Not mine.

For some reason the thought made me very sad. Maybe because it reminded me that other than Rita, Fred and Ben, I didn't have family. One of the hard things about losing Blake was that it was like losing my family all over again. It brought back shades of losing my parents. How even though Rita and I knew we'd always be a family, when they died it was as if our circle had been broken, flattened out into a straight line that we couldn't put back together again.

At one point I almost contemplated telling Jean Luc I couldn't go.

There would be too many questions.

My parents were dead. Yes, I had one sister and a son. The son's father?

We're not divorced yet, but yes, I'm sleeping with your son.

Jean Luc told me in the French culture people did not ask such vulgar questions because they only served to embarrass the one being interrogated.

Speaking of questions, I had some for him.

Why did he want me to meet the folks?

What did this mean?

I couldn't ask, of course, for fear of being *vulgar*. Or maybe it was for fear of hearing what he'd say.

If he was introducing me for the reason most middle-aged men introduced women to their parents—I just wasn't ready for that yet, but I didn't know how to tell him that without making things weird between us.

So, that Sunday, I took out the cream cashmere sweater and navy trousers I'd worn on the airplane; donned my pearls, which I hadn't worn since arriving at the Delacroix Centre, and after smoothing my hair into a nice, neat chignon, I plucked out the errant gray. I was way overdue for a color and cut, but I hadn't noticed because of the camouflaging effect of wild curls *au naturel*.

My old uniform. It felt strange and looked stranger, as if I were staring in the mirror at someone I didn't recognize. But this was the only way I knew how to cope with meeting the parents.

When Jean Luc arrived at my door, dressed head to toe in his trademark black, he did a double take before hugging me.

"This is a different look for you."

I picked up the bouquet of hydrangeas I'd purchased for his mother and held them to my nose.

"You've never seen me dressed up," I said.

"I prefer you undressed." He buried his nose in the base of my neck. "Mmm, you smell nice."

He pulled away and looked at me. "It's just—it is not you. Your hair is pulled back so tightly it looks as if it hurts."

He reached around and his big hands fumbled with the band that held my hair, but I pulled out of his reach before he could free it.

"What are you doing?"

"I am returning you to the woman I know. To the woman with the curls. This one looks too uptight."

I was stunned. I couldn't help thinking of how Blake always preferred me to pull my hair back. Jean Luc caught my face in his hands and tilted it up to his.

"I love…"

His words trailed off, and the look on his face was soft as a caress. My stomach swirled in a slow spiral.

"I love your curls," he finally said.

As I let him reach back and free my hair, I realized I was glad he'd said *curls*.

I couldn't wait to call Rita the next day while Jean Luc was out. I guess I wanted to gloat since she'd been so sure he was going to sleep with me and go straight back to Matilde.

"I'm just glad I wore my pearls." I paced while I talked to her.

"That fancy, huh?"

"His parents' *house* was an eighteenth-century mansion near the Trocadéro. Rita, it was the most gorgeous place I'd ever seen. The dining room had these huge casement windows that framed this incredible view of the Eiffel Tower. It was unreal. I didn't think people really lived like that."

"So what were the folks like?"

The canvas on my easel caught my eye and I stopped in front of it, picked up my brush and dabbed some paint on the portrait of a Pigalle hooker. Despite the amount of time I'd been spending with Jean Luc, I'd managed to keep working and had finished fifteen paintings in the Pigalle series.

"*Maman* was very proper," I said. "Small and *très élégante*. Meticulously dressed. She wore her pearls, too. *Papa* was tall and handsome. That's where Jean Luc gets his looks. Strong resemblance."

"So does this mean things are serious?"

"No." I set down my brush and resumed pacing. "Absolutely not."

"Does Jean Luc know this?"

I couldn't work, I was distracted by a certain restlessness that had me throwing big gobs of paint on the canvas.

No rhyme.

No reason.

I was just too restless to stay inside and paint.

The Parisian wind told stories as it gusted in through the open eastern window and raced out in a cross-breeze through the French doors on the western side, only to circle around and flirt with me again.

It caressed my cheek, kissed my throat, whispered in my ear that there was so much out there that I needed to see. I closed my eyes against its lusty invitation and tried to resist, but I couldn't sit still for long.

Jean Luc must have picked up on my restlessness because he turned up at my door just as I was getting ready to go out.

I hated to admit it, but I really wished I hadn't taken the time to fuss with my hair because if I'd left five minutes earlier, I would have missed him and I could have taken my walk.

But he walked into my studio that beautiful morning and said, "Get your purse and lock your studio. I have something I want to show you."

"I was just getting ready to go out," I said.

"Where were you going?"

Why do you need to know?

"Nowhere, really. Just out for a walk."

God, I was a terrible person for feeling this way. He was so wonderful to me.

He led me to a gorgeous, silver Mercedes parked outside the center and opened the passenger-side door for me.

"Where are we going?"

"It is a surprise."

I played along, telling myself to relax when my body responded with prickles of irritation as he slid his hand underneath my skirt and up my thigh, teasing his fingers along the elastic of my underwear.

I closed my legs and angled them away from him. "Okay, Casanova, keep both hands on the wheel."

PMS?

Oversaturation?

I glanced over at him, his profile like a European god, and I decided it had to be PMS. Usually, one look at those eyes, those lips, those shoulders cured anything that ailed me.

It had to be PMS. Just relax.

"Jean Luc, we've been on the highway for an hour. Where are we going?"

He slanted a glance at me and smiled. My heart did a little two-step. That was more like it.

"Cannes."

"Cannes? What? That's at the other end of the country."

"I know. I have some business to tend to and I thought you might like to accompany me."

Annoyance stomped out the awareness that had bloomed in my belly. "Why didn't you tell me so that I could at least pack a toothbrush?"

"I have extra toothbrushes."

"I'll need a change of clothes."

He shot me a devilish grin and put his hand on my thigh again. "As far as I am concerned, my love, you won't need clothing."

I stared out the window, at war with myself, irritated because he didn't even give me the courtesy of asking whether I wanted to go. He must have sensed my irritation because we rode for miles in silence, past farm country and lavender fields. Finally, after I'd fumed enough, I convinced myself the impromptu trip was an adventure and forced myself into a better mood.

It was almost eight-thirty by the time we arrived at his family's Villa Angeline. A house with a name—actually it was a mansion from *who knows what century*, perched high on a Côte d'Azur cliff overlooking the Mediterranean Sea.

We stood on a balcony over the pool, looking down at the sea. The waxing moon shone like quicksilver on the water far below. Any residual irritation I felt earlier evaporated.

It really was mind-boggling to get in a car and end up on the other side of the country with only my purse and the clothes on my back. I thought of the green monster and the other baggage I'd dragged all the way to Paris and wanted to laugh.

If Rita could only see me now.

Jean Luc and I sat at a table on the terrace sipping champagne by candlelight and feasting on petits fours with caviar, crudités, fresh figs, foie gras, bread and an assortment of meats and cheeses Jean Luc had packed in a cooler and brought with us. He'd put so much thought into this trip. This surprise for me.

"When we go into town, I'd like to buy a bathing suit."

"You don't need one. It's very private up here."

"I'll need something if we go to the beach."

"Oh, did you want to do that?"

"Of course. I can't come all this way and not stick my feet in the Mediterranean Sea."

"Then I shall see that it happens." He reached out and took my hand. I couldn't decide if he was the most romantic man I'd ever met or controlling and chauvinistic for bringing me here this way.

Oh! What was wrong with me?

I stared at our fingers entwined. Things were going so well. Why was I spoiling it for myself by feeling like this? I'd always thought of happiness as a beautiful flower. So incredibly fragile and fine, and so short-lived. I guess from the moment Blake and I got married I was waiting for the bloom to fall off. Whether I realized it or not, I always felt as if he was just out of my grasp.

Now that I have a man who is treating me the way I *should* be treated, I feel like I can't get away fast enough. I hated the melancholy that was choking me.

It was just one of those days. All relationships had them. Never mind that this mood, these feelings of riding a careening cart rushing along out of control, started shortly after he invited me to dinner with his parents.

It had been a long tiring day of travel and I was exhausted. *Snap out of it, Annabelle.*

"How long are we staying?" I asked. "My son, Ben, arrives in three days."

"Not to worry. We can spend two days here and I will deliver you in time to receive him. We can pick him up together."

Hmm... I hadn't thought about that and I wasn't sure how I felt about it, either. What would Ben think of his mother getting involved before the divorce was final?

"While we're here we can get you some supplies if you would like to work," he said. "And did you realize your artist, Camille Deveau, spent the last years of her life in Cannes?"

Oh! That's right. "I read about that. It was just a brief passage in the biography, but I guess I was so swept away by the surprise of this spontaneous trip, I completely forgot about it."

Don't be bitchy.

"I thought you might like to have a look around her old neighborhood. How about if we do that tomorrow?"

I smiled and looked at the kind, beautiful man sitting across from me. Wanting to say, *You're divorced. How can you be so sure about life and love after losing yourself to someone and having it end badly?*

Instead, I sank into my chair and gazed up at the star-dotted indigo sky, breathing in the heady, salty air.

"I must go out and take care of something tonight. How about if you run yourself a bath upstairs and relax while I'm gone?"

It was almost ten o'clock.

"You have to go out tonight?"

He nodded. "It really can't wait. I will be gone about an hour, but when I get back, I promise to bring dessert."

He smiled that smile that could persuade me to dive off the hillside into the sea below. Then he led me upstairs and showed me the master bedroom.

It was decorated in traditional French white and gold, with expensive-looking antiques. The floor was herringbone parquet, topped with what I was sure were priceless Oriental rugs. The crowning glory was an immense four-poster bed, with a little wooden step so that you could climb in without having to hoist yourself up.

The bathroom was all marble, chrome and mirrors. Considerably more modern than the bedroom, and bigger than the first apartment I shared with a roommate when I was in college. The marble tub could have comfortably seated six.

But it was all for me.

Before he left, he ran my bath, dumping in gardenia-scented bath salts and attaching an air-filled pillow for me to rest my head on before he undressed me.

"Are you sure there's nothing I can do to persuade you to get in here with me?" If we could just get to that place where we connected so well I was sure everything would be fine.

He bit his bottom lip and closed his eyes. "You have no idea how you tempt me. But I must go. The sooner I go the sooner I will be back."

He left me to soak alone in that big, beautiful tub with air jets that kept the water warm. I felt like a princess for the first five minutes, but then the gardenia scent of the bath salts transported me back to my studio in Orlando, which made me think of the day Rita brought me the slides and the application for the residency trip.

Family.

Rita, Fred and Ben.

The quantity didn't matter, really, it was the quality of the relationship that counted. We shared a closer bond than some enormous families.

A pang of sadness morphed into homesickness, and I realized this was one of those times when I would have called my sister. But I didn't even have my cell phone with me. It was in Paris charging on the little café table by the kitchen.

The melancholy blue seeped into my pores, but I took a deep breath and blew it away, sinking deeper in the hot water, thinking about what I would have said if I could have talked to Rita.

I must have dozed as I steeped because I awoke with a start. For a moment I was disoriented and didn't remember where I was.

My skin was so waterlogged it was pruny.

I sat up, hit the button to stop the water jets and looked around. I had the eeriest feeling someone had been watching me. The bathroom door was cracked a bit, and I couldn't remember if Jean Luc had closed it all the way when he left.

Shuddering at the thought of being alone in this big, old unfamiliar house I climbed out of the tub and pulled on the white terry robe hanging on the back of the door.

I crept out of the bathroom hesitantly, with my ears trained to see if I could hear anything.

A door slammed somewhere downstairs, causing a little exclamation to jump to life in my throat.

I walked to the top of the staircase and listened for Jean Luc's footsteps, but all was quiet.

"Jean Luc?"

The only answer was the sound of my pounding heart.

CHAPTER 14

I locked myself in the bedroom for a terrifying half hour. There was a telephone on the nightstand, but I had no idea how to dial French emergency.

Even if I'd known how, I had no idea how to ask for the police in French. I didn't have my lexicon with me. It, too, was back in Paris along with my passport.

All sorts of morbid thoughts flooded my mind.

The old house was just creepy. If I believed in ghosts my imagination would have really gotten carried away with me.

But I didn't believe in ghosts. Actually, ghosts were nothing compared to the monsters men could be.

I thought about the old cliché *If something's too good to be true it usually is*. Of course, it was happening again. Jean Luc *was* too good to be true. Men never did turn out to be who they claimed to be.

That was the banana peel that sent my exhausted, overactive mind slipping and sliding on a panicky collision course.

I sat down on the bed.

I'd known him for a few weeks, but did I really know

him? Oh my God, what if he was some kind of deranged psychopath who used his charm and good looks to lure unsuspecting women into traps so he could kill them? Maybe that's what happened to Matilde.

Oh my God, I hadn't seen her since that day in Pigalle. It was as if she'd vanished.

Oh my God, I could see the headline—Mediocre Middle-aged Artist Disappears In Paris. Jacques Jauvert would insist on the word mediocre, that way he'd be able to inform the world just how bad my art was.

Okay, calm down. That's ridiculous. You've met his parents. He teaches at the Beaux-Arts. But I *knew* I heard a door slam. Someone was in here or had been in here.

Jean Luc said this place sat vacant most of the time, except for the caretakers. It was full of beautiful antiques and artwork. A burglar's dream.

I picked up a heavy silver candlestick off the bureau and sat next to the phone. If someone tried to break down the door, I'd dial O and take my chance that they'd *parlez-vous Anglais*. Never mind that I had no idea where the hell I was other than in Cannes.

How could I be so stupid letting him bring me here like this? I should have made him turn the car around.

I tried dialing Rita, just to tell her I loved her and in case I turned up dead she should tell Ben I loved him, too. But I couldn't remember the country code—was it zero, one, one or one, zero, one—all those damn numbers.

I was just about to take my chances and ask the operator to place the call for me when I heard a car pull into the driveway. I ran to the window and saw Jean Luc getting out of his silver Mercedes.

Relief flooded through me.

Feeling vaguely foolish about my earlier thoughts of him as a psycho-killer, I wanted to meet him at the door and throw myself into his arms, but what if I walked in on the intruder? They'd hear Jean Luc coming in and would have enough time to get away. I stood on the far side of the room clutching the candlestick, waiting for him to come up to me.

He tried to open the door, but it was locked. "Annabelle? It's me. The bedroom door's locked. Will you let me in, please?"

I did and he took one look and said, "What's the matter?"

I was shaking so hard the candlestick waved back and forth.

"Someone was here, in the house." My voice shook, too, and I was afraid I would buckle under all the emotion.

In the split second before he gathered me in his arms I saw a flash of panic in his eyes. If I hadn't been looking at him at that precise moment I would have missed it, and even though I had started to feel a little better about the situation, that little spark reignited the fear that something just wasn't right.

"What do you mean someone was here? Are you all right?"

With my cheek pressed against his chest, I told him how I'd dozed off in the tub, and though I didn't see anyone, I felt a presence and heard a door slam. "I know it wasn't just my imagination."

I waited for him to laugh and explain it away. To say it was probably the caretaker or that the old house was drafty and made all kinds of creaks and groans, sounds like doors slamming. He didn't say any of those things, and when I pulled out of his arms, his mouth was set in a grim line.

Panic erupted in me all over again. So *maybe* he wasn't a psychopath, but I had no idea what kind of *business* he was conducting in Cannes in the middle of the night. What if his business was not on the up-and-up—drugs, money laundering, illegal weapons, white slavery—

Oh my God, this was how women were sold into slavery, never to be heard of again.

"I want to go back to Paris," I said.

He nodded. "We'll leave in the morning. We're both exhausted. Let's get some sleep."

After driving all this way, why was he so quick to agree? Why wasn't he trying to explain away the situation?

"No, I want to go now. I don't care if you have to put me on a train. I am not staying the night in this house."

* * *

We drove straight through and got back to Paris at six o'clock in the morning.

Jean Luc was not happy about my insisting we leave, but when I threatened to call a cab to take me to the train station (thank God he didn't call my bluff), he said, "I don't know that there is a train at this hour. You are being ridiculous."

I insisted, saying he had a lot of nerve just whisking me down here like this without asking me if I had engagements or if I even wanted to go. How dare he just assume I had nothing better to do. Everything I'd been feeling since I'd awakened to find myself in this lousy frame of mind came pouring out.

The grave hurt and insult of my words were apparent in his sigh.

He complied.

It was the longest eight hours of my life.

When we pulled up in front of the studio, I was surprised and relieved when he accepted my offer to make him coffee. I hoped that meant he'd stay and we'd crawl into my bed and hold each other while we slept so we could wake up and laugh about the whole fiasco.

He'd get a kick out of how I momentarily thought he'd kidnapped me and taken me down there for—God, I couldn't even remember. It all seemed so ridiculous now.

We were both silent as I measured water into the French press, transferred it to the kettle and set the water to boil. I arranged croissants (now two days old), grapes and melon slices on a plate.

I took out the new yellow linen place mats I'd purchased from the little rue Cler linen shop and put them on the café table by the kitchen window. I finished setting the table with my new blue cloth napkins and the flatware.

Blake always thought cloth table linens were impractical, so I never used them. Since arriving in France I'd made it a personal code never to use paper napkins on my table. I poured cream into a tiny porcelain pitcher, set out plates, juice glasses, coffee mugs the size of cereal bowls and all the while was aware of Jean Luc silently watching me, his arms folded across his chest and a grim, tired look on his face.

The kettle whistled. I poured the water over the coffee in the press pot, stirred it and gestured toward the table.

"Sit down."

He eyed the table, then looked back at me. "I think we need to spend some time apart, Anna."

His words hit like a slap, and my hand jerked. A tidal wave of water and grounds sloshed over the side onto the countertop. I grabbed a towel to wipe up the mess, thinking maybe if I acted like I didn't hear him he'd pretend he didn't say what he just said.

No such luck.

"You need to prepare for your son's visit, and I should be busy organizing the final jury examination of my students. I need to be fresh so I can give them the attention they deserve."

I wanted to tell him I only needed a day to prepare for Ben and ask him how he would've managed to organize the examination if we'd stayed in Cannes for another two days.

The questions rolled around in my mind like a tumbleweed getting tangled with absurd phrases like *Oh my God, he's a psycho-killer; this is how women are sold into slavery;* and *I want to go back to Paris now.* I couldn't unknot the words, "Please don't go." I just stood dumbly staring into the black abyss of my French press, stirring the coffee.

"I will talk to you soon," he said as he walked up behind me and brushed a featherlight kiss on the top of my head.

This time I knew without a doubt the door I heard shutting was not a figment of my imagination.

The first day's separation reminded me that I was a strong, self-sufficient, independent woman. In fact, I was enjoying the time to myself. I'd missed this alone time. I painted a little and lay in the sun, totally nude, thank you very much. I even went and got my hair colored and trimmed (just a smidgen because I liked how long it was getting).

I felt like a million bucks.

He was probably missing me already.

* * *

The second day, I painted with the front door and all my windows open so I had a clear view of his studio—or should I say so that when he arrived at his studio *he* could see that I was doing perfectly fine, that I was a *talented*, strong, self-sufficient, independent woman.

When he hadn't shown up by four o'clock on the second day, I took the metro over to his apartment and put a note on his door.

> I hope everything is going well as you organize your students' final exams. Please let me know if you're still planning on going with me to the airport to pick up Ben.
> Anna

Maybe I should have signed it *Love, Anna*. Nah, I was the one who had made the first move. *Anna*, plain and simple, was good enough.

I still hadn't heard from Jean Luc on day number three, the day Ben would arrive. I awoke thinking the standoff had gone on long enough.

Okay, fine. I was willing to throw in the towel and admit that I'd acted a little crazy. He could blame it on my being an "uptight American," if it made him feel better.

I'd tell him I was scared. Of us. Of where this relationship was heading, and I thought I had just broken through the other side of those fears.

I missed him. Plain and simple. I didn't want to spend any more time apart.

My son was arriving today and I wanted the two men I loved to—

Oh my God, there it was.

The "L" word.

I sat up in bed and covered my mouth with my hand as if I could shove the word back in before it made itself comfortable in my vocabulary, but it was already out. It had been out there for a long time, and that's what was wrong.

I loved him.

But it was okay.

It was more than okay.

It was time he knew it.

I had no idea what his student jury examinations entailed. Or if he'd even begun them. He could be finished for all I knew. It was worth a shot to go over to his apartment to see if I could catch him.

I didn't waste time showering for fear it would mean the difference between my finding him at home and missing him. I just pulled on my clothes, grabbed my purse and went.

I punched in the code to his building and walked up to his place on the third floor.

The message I'd left him yesterday still stuck out of the crevice between the door and the jamb.

Oh. He hadn't even been home.

Hmm. This was interesting. I wondered where he'd been if he wasn't sleeping here or at the studio.

I stood there a moment battling with a mental monster that pointed to all kinds of possibilities I didn't like, that twisted my stomach and made my heart ache.

I took down the note because it was irrelevant at that point. Obviously, Jean Luc wouldn't be taking me to meet Ben. But that was okay, because going by myself I could focus on Ben.

Really, it was better this way. In the meantime, I'd give Jean Luc the benefit of the doubt until I could ask him just where he'd been. Perhaps he still had business in Cannes.

Then why didn't he tell me? Why did he say the bit about the student exams?

I'd just turned to leave when I heard voices on the landing below; a deep, sexy French accent that started a passionate fluttering in my belly.

He was home.

But he wasn't alone.

A lilting French female voice floated up the stairs ahead of their footsteps. I thought I recognized the voice.

But I wasn't sure.

Until she laughed.

And then I knew.

Matilde.

I bit my lip until I could feel it throb in time with my pulse. So *that's* where he'd been for the past two days. Final student jury examinations, my ass.

He'd been with *her*.

Each footstep brought them closer to the third floor and made my heart pound harder. I looked around, trying to decide what to do. The only way out was to walk down the stairs past them.

I'd be damned if I'd let Jean Luc know I'd come over here ready to make up. That I— They'd both probably laugh in my face. *Stupid American*.

I took the only other possible option. I climbed up to the next floor to wait and watch.

CHAPTER 15

I straightened the studio and set out fresh linens to make up the couch for Ben's bed later that night. He only had four days in Paris because he was taking summer school to get ahead on his credits and only had a week between terms. Factor in two days spent flying and a day for jet-lag recovery before jumping into class and that left a net total of four days to see Paris.

It was definitely better that Jean Luc was not in the picture vying for my attention. My stomach twisted at the memory of him unlocking his apartment door and holding it open for Matilde to enter. That's all I saw. The door shut and I beelined out of the building.

Bile rose in the back of my throat. I took a deep breath and willed my stomach to settle. I had too much to do today.

First order of business: Clear the studio of every trace of Jean Luc.

Second order of business: No moping over Jean Luc.

Third order of business: No mention of Jean Luc to Ben.

Fourth order of business: Quit thinking of Jean Luc!

I hadn't uttered a single word about him to Ben (and made Rita promise to be quiet, too) for precisely this reason.

Maybe somewhere in the recesses of my heart, I knew the relationship would end this way.

With Matilde.

Just like Rita predicted. I'd been so cocksure it wouldn't.

I trusted him.

He lied.

I was beginning to see a relationship pattern.

I trusted men.

They lied.

I spied the blue package of his Gitane cigarettes on the kitchen counter, and images of him in the stairwell with *the blonde* skittered through my mind. I closed my eyes against the ensuing ache.

This *would* happen right before Ben's visit.

Bad timing.

Bad judgment.

If it was destined to end, better he excused himself before meeting Ben.

I took a cigarette out of the pack, rolled it across my palm, then lifted it to my nose to inhale the tobacco that reminded me so much of him. I'd always been turned off by smokers, but there was something earthily sensual about his lips when he inhaled. Like foreign poetry.

Fifth order of business: Quit being pathetic.

I lifted the unlit cylinder to my lips, touched it to the tip of my tongue. The unfiltered end tasted of his raw, smoky essence.

Amazing how our tastes adapted to the whims of our hearts.

I snapped the cigarette in half, dumped the rest of the pack on the counter and finished off the job, sweeping the carnage into the trash.

Flopping down on the couch with a *pfff*, I forced all the air from my lungs and buried my face in my hands.

If I was going to cry, I'd better get on with it. Just get it over with now. Because I had exactly two hours to wallow and subsequently stash my feelings before my son arrived.

I sat staring into the blackness of my palms, waiting for the tears to burn my eyes and swim to the surface, but my hands smelled like broken cigarettes.

Like broken dreams?

No. I looked up. My dreams still belonged to me. That was one thing I did right this time.

I glanced around the modest studio, which looked different through my sad eyes. My gaze locked with Jean Luc's intense stare peering at me from *The Bed* painting hanging on the wall in front of me. My heart twisted.

He'd hung the canvas the afternoon after we first made love. He said such a special painting deserved a place of honor.

It was the only painting hanging on the wall; the rest of my work was lined up around the room on the paint-spattered wooden floor, propped up against the white stucco walls. The bizarre images looked like portals into some strange alternate universe.

As a whole, the body of work was about as different from the chaste flowers I used to paint as a hooker was from a debutante.

I raked my hair out of my eyes. God, what would Ben think of his mother now?

His dad was gay and his mom had gone off the deep end glorifying the seamy side of Paris. To hell with *La Tour Eiffel*, give me the whores and cross-dressers of Par-ee.

I swallowed hard. How come my work didn't seem so odious until I tried to see it through my son's eyes?

My assessment of the studio came full circle back to *The Bed*.

If Ben was sleeping on the couch, I couldn't have him staring at my former lover in the throes of passionate sex with a woman who was—a thinly veiled version of me.

Not that Ben would know, but still.

I took the canvas off the wall and carried the huge painting into the bedroom, my eyes searching for a place to stash it. The closet was too small, the bureau was flush against the wall and too heavy to pull out by myself. I could have stashed the canvas under the bed, but the mattress was on one of those solid platforms that didn't offer any storage space underneath.

I thought about hiding it at the back of a stack of can-vases, but it was by far the largest painting in the studio; besides, the first thing people did when they walked into an artist's studio was to start looking at the work.

It annoyed me. People didn't walk into a writer's office and start reading their work in progress. For some reason painting lacked the privacy afforded to other creative work. For want of anything else to do with it, I turned it backward and propped it against the bedroom wall.

I went back to the living room to see if there was anything I missed, anything on which I should exercise parental discretion and remove.

The place really was small; fine for one person, but housing two was going to be a challenge.

As tight as Rita and I were, we'd have been at each other's throats in such close quarters. Especially with one of us sleeping on the couch.

Habit made me glance out the window to see if Jean Luc's studio was open. It wasn't, of course. He was probably still with *her*.

Matilde is not my lover.

Her work with me is finished.

Liar.

I should take *The Bed* and nail it to his studio door. Let him have it and all the memories associated with it. Let him explain to Matilde about the woman he was making love to in the painting. But I didn't know when he'd be back and I didn't want to take the chance of it sitting there when Ben arrived.

What's that, Mom?

Oh, just a painting, Ben. In Paris, you find artwork in the most unlikely places.

The woman looks familiar.

Nobody you know, believe me.

I turned my back to the window and picked the wilting blooms out of the bouquet of freesias in the vase on the table. Too bad Ben and I weren't staying in Benoît Bernard's place like Rita and I did.

I lifted a dying blossom to my nose. It smelled of decay and perfume. A once-beautiful flower just past its prime.

Why not? Why couldn't we stay there?

He'd want to see my studio, of course, but maybe if I keep him busy enough…

Oh, gee, where did the time go, Ben? Too bad we didn't have a chance to see the studio. But you've seen one studio, you've seen them all.

Yeah, right. We'd cross that bridge when we came to it.

There was always the chance that the apartment wouldn't be available. What then?

How much to stay at the Ritz?

Okay, on my budget we'd have to settle for the Parisian equivalent of a Motel 6.

As long as we were anyplace but here.

I called Rita and got Benoît Bernard's phone number. I left a message on his answering service, and he returned my call within the hour.

Good timing, he said. While he couldn't vacate the apartment in time for us to stay there that night, he said he welcomed the excuse to go to his place in Provence for a long weekend. We could have it for three nights starting tomorrow.

Perfect. Ben and I could take a quick overnight trip somewhere—Versailles? Giverny? I'd have to see what I could arrange in short order.

Monsieur Bernard said he would leave the key with Étienne at the crêpe restaurant.

Oh. God. That's right. Étienne.

I hadn't seen him since *that day*.

I had a flash of total clarity when I realized I'd made the right decision not sleeping with him. At least that was one thing I'd done right.

Étienne was a grown man. I'd give him the benefit of the doubt he'd conduct himself accordingly. In fact, he was probably already engaged to another middle-aged American woman who could give him his green card.

I hoped so.

I'd be cordial, but not *overly* friendly. Nothing to betray to Ben what almost happened. After all, I was his mother. I wasn't even divorced from his father yet.

Since Ben and I weren't staying at the studio, I decided I'd wasted enough time cleaning and quickly changed gears. I packed an overnight bag, and took the early train to the airport, arriving about an hour before Ben's flight. It gave me time to check train schedules and map out a plan.

By the time his plane arrived we probably wouldn't be able to make the last train for Versailles, but Giverny would work.

Yes, that was it. I'd always wanted to see Monet's home and gardens. Too bad I didn't pack my easel.

I'd always been emotional—I cried when I was happy, I cried when I was sad. I cried when Ben emerged through the security gates. Seeing him felt like someone had sent a *rescuer* to save me, and I hugged him as if he were my life support.

My son.

"You're here," I said, holding him by the shoulders. "I have missed you so much."

"I missed you, too, Mom. Please don't cry."

I swiped at my eyes and nose, embarrassed at losing control. "I'm sorry. I've just missed you."

I hugged him again.

At Charles de Gaulle, international passengers get their baggage before they enter the airport's common areas. With that taken care of, we had just enough time to grab a bite to eat and make it to the Gare Saint-Lazare where we bought our tickets and boarded the train for Giverny.

"I know you're tired, but I thought we'd do this first so you could ease into your whirlwind tour of Paris."

It made sense.

He had dark circles under his eyes, and I wanted to gather him in my arms and let him sleep on my shoulder the way he did when he was a little boy.

"Why don't we just stay at your studio?"

I waved a hand nonchalantly. "Oh, it's too small for the two of us. Plus, this is your first time in Paris. I want everything to be perfect."

Little did he know.

The trip took about an hour, and I encouraged Ben to sleep after his long flight.

As I sat there looking at this man-child who was my son, my heart was so full, frankly I didn't care where we stayed, just as long as we were together. I was so glad to see my baby.

"You look so grown-up," I said.

He rolled his eyes. "Me? What about you? I mean, you don't look grown-up, you look…you look great. Younger, I think." He smiled at me. "Your hair's so long. I don't think I've ever seen you wear it this way. What did you do to it?"

I shrugged. "Not much. That's the beauty of it."

After about an hour, the train chugged into the station at Vernon. We took a ten-minute cab ride to the little Norman village of Giverny.

I'd secured us a room at a bed-and-breakfast called Le Coin des Artistes, which translated to the Artists' Corner. Located right on the rue Claude Monet, it was just down from the famous painter's home and gardens.

The B and B used to be an old café and general store, but the proprietor, Madame Laurence, had transformed it into a quaint four-guest room bed-and-breakfast.

She showed us to a double room. Ben swore he was

too keyed up to take a nap, so we strolled down to the
Hôtel Baudy, a place I'd heard almost as much about as
Monet's house.

In the late nineteenth century, the Hôtel Baudy was
dubbed "the hotel of the American painters."

How appropriate, I thought as we chose a table with
a yellow umbrella under the lime trees, by a low hedge
that cordoned off the outer bounds of the terrace from
a lush green field. It was approaching five o'clock and
most of the tables were available. The rush of day tourists who came in to see Monet's house was starting to
thin.

A small woman with dark hair handed us menus and
said something in French I thought was, *I'll be right
back.*

I studied the menu. "The drinking age in France is
sixteen," I said. "Do you want to share a bottle of wine?"

Ben's gaze snapped to mine. "Really?"

"Well, we don't have to. I just thought—"

"Sure." He squared his shoulders and sat back, looking way too much like a man.

He was equal parts Blake and me. He had Blake's fair
hair, but definitely my eyes and nose. The set of his
jaw—that was all Blake, especially when I asked him if
he'd spoken to his father.

"No."

Yes, just like his father. The word was delivered to
end the conversation before it began. I didn't want to
spoil the night so I didn't push.

After the server took our order—the salad with cold smoked salmon for me, the beef bourguignon for Ben, a bottle of Beaujolais for us to share—a hush fell between us.

As I gazed at the Hôtel Baudy, now only a restaurant, they no longer let rooms to guests, I could feel Ben's distress emanating in waves.

I was sorry I'd mentioned Blake. I was just hoping they'd made some progress while I was gone. I hadn't talked to Blake since I'd been in Paris and chose not to waste my short weekly calls with Ben on the subject, so I didn't know.

It seemed as if with each passing moment, Ben sank deeper into silent despair.

No. This wouldn't do.

"I read that when Monet came to Giverny, the Hôtel Baudy was only a small place for travelers to eat and freshen up," I said, hoping to reclaim the light, relaxed mood we'd enjoyed a few minutes ago.

Ben nodded and stared somewhere over my shoulder.

"They built the hotel after all the American Impressionists started coming here." I gestured to the pink stucco building across the narrow rue Claude Monet from the terrace where we sat. There were sidewalks in some American cities wider than the street and I wondered what happened if two cars traveling in opposite directions met each other.

"The hotel has a rich history," I continued, keeping my voice light. "There's supposed to be a magical garden and artists' studio around back. If you're not too tired maybe we can take a look at it after we eat."

"Sure, Mom." Unenthused.

"It's been preserved to look as it did when the Baudys built it back in the late 1800s for all the Americans who came here to paint. You know how they discovered this place?"

My zeal must have sounded as canned as it felt, because Ben simply raised his eyebrows at my question.

God, I didn't blame him. I sounded like a travel guide, but it was better than contemplating the ghost of the Blake we both thought we knew and once loved.

"It was because of the painter William Metcalf. He fell in love with this place and went back to Paris and told all his American friends. In fact, when he first stopped in for a meal at Baudys', Madame Baudy was afraid of him. She said he was a burly hirsute beast with no manners who spoke gibberish."

The server delivered the wine. I lifted my glass.

"A toast to you and Paris." We clinked glasses.

"I don't know if I'll ever be able to forgive him," Ben finally said. He rested his chin on his fist and looked so forlorn I almost couldn't bear it.

I touched his arm, wishing I could do something to fix this. "It doesn't change his love for you, honey."

Ben snorted as if the very thought was disgusting. "Yeah, but what does it mean about his love for you? Did he ever love you, Mom? Why did he even marry you?"

Those were the million-dollar questions. The questions that had sent me "Faraway" searching for answers.

I stroked his arm, surprised that for the first time contemplating the answers didn't leave me seething with anger or on the verge of tears. "I've asked myself those questions so many times, Ben, and the conclusion I've finally reached is that everything happens for a reason. Sometimes we don't know what that reason is, but we just have to go forward in blind faith. If I hadn't met your dad, I wouldn't have you. Being your mother is worth any price. If I can forgive him, I hope you can, too."

Ben contemplated his wine for a moment, then lifted his glass to mine.

"Nice thought, Mom, but easier said than done."

Just give it time, Ben.

After dinner we wandered back to the Hôtel Baudy garden. The replica of the nineteenth-century artists' studio sat so still and perfect with its ochre-washed walls and paint-spattered floor it looked as if a working artist had just stepped away for a bite to eat and would return to resume his work.

Several easels held canvases in various stages of progress; a swag of ivy had infiltrated the roof's far left corner, embedding itself in the plaster; pieces of pottery and sculpture lay scattered in random groupings around the space; under a magnificent window that stretched nearly the length of the right wall, a low, red-painted workbench held jewel-toned jars of pigment, paint palettes, jars of crusty old brushes and an open wooden painter's box.

It was as if we'd stepped back in time to a simpler era. I looked out the dusty, weathered window and squinted my eyes. I could almost see the haunting images the American painters came here to capture more than a century ago: the lush flora and fauna, the children playing in the garden, the well dressed ladies with delicate parasols basking in the splendor of the blossoms.

Ben and I strolled side by side, in companionable silence, and I thought about what I'd said to him.

If I can forgive him, I hope you can, too.

Forgiveness.

Had I forgiven Blake? I hadn't even considered it until now. Really, it was the first step in the long journey toward healing.

The garden was laden with perfumed roses growing in enchanting abandon. Rustic perennials installed themselves under the canopy of trees, and vines snaked their way up the trunks. Daisies and hypericum guarded a winding path that led up to the summit of a hill.

It was so quiet it almost felt as if we were the only two people in the village. Just us and the souls of all those long-ago painters. People just like me and Camille Deveau who had lived and loved, celebrated great joys and endured unbearable heartbreak.

They'd all lived and loved and dealt with their share of betrayal and sadness, and the world went on after they were gone. Despite it all, they left behind their art and their flowers and their buildings that once rang with their laughter and tears.

The day I'd learned of Blake's betrayal, I was on my way to see the traveling collection of Monet's water-lily paintings. I never got to see them. Because of that, here I stood in the very place they originated. What a long, roundabout journey getting here.

I was starting to believe some things really did happen for a reason. So who was I to fancy that the pain I'd suffered was any worse than the anguish of those brave souls who came before me? They made it, didn't they? Perhaps some were better because of it.

As we walked back to Le Coin des Artistes, I stopped to inhale the sweet scent of an ancient rosebush bent under the weight of its blooms.

In a note that drifted in on the breeze, I closed my eyes and imagined Camille Deveau whispering, *The next step of your long, roundabout journey is learning to forgive yourself.*

CHAPTER 16

When Ben and I returned to Paris, I was nervous about getting the key to the apartment from Étienne. I sent Ben across the street into the Nicholas shop to buy us a bottle of wine. Since he wasn't of age at home, I knew he'd get a kick out of being able to make the purchase legally here.

It also meant I could approach Étienne alone since I had no idea what he'd say or do. I mustered all my confidence and approached the crêpe restaurant.

He wasn't at the counter. I had to ask some guy I didn't recognize, if he knew where Étienne was. I wondered if he was one of the guys I saw out front the day I first arrived.

Less than a minute later, Étienne walked out from the back dangling the key between his right index finger and thumb. He stared at me for a moment, unsmiling, before he said, "Ah, *bonjour*, American Woman."

He leaned on the counter and made exaggerated glances up and down the street. "Where is your man-friend?"

My breath escaped in a rush that sounded more irritated than I'd intended. "Étienne, I'm here with my son. The key. Please?"

I held out my hand, but he held it just out of my reach. Was he going to drag this out until Ben came? For God's sake I hoped not.

"Where is he?" Étienne asked.

I wondered if he meant Ben or Jean Luc, so I took my chances. "My son is over at Nicholas across the street. If you're nice I'll introduce you to him. But only if you're nice."

"Is he by himself or is *You-Know-What* with him?"

I laughed. "You mean *You-Know-Who?*"

"I mean your *manfriend.* It is same thing, no?"

"Not exactly." *You-Know-What. Another priceless Étienne-ism. I'd have to remember it.* "No, my *manfriend* is not with us." For a second I considered telling Étienne that Jean Luc and I were finished, but then decided against it when the numbness I'd resurrected for the duration of Ben's visit started to fade.

What was the use of opening that vein of conversation?

Étienne pursed his lips and stroked his clean-shaven chin as if considering his options. Then he leaned in and dropped the key in my palm.

I kissed him on the cheek. "Thank you, French Boy."

He smiled. "If you ever leave *You-Know-What,* I will be right here."

I shook my head in mock disgust. "Until you find

yourself another American woman and go off to the U.S. with her to open your restaurant."

He sighed dramatically and patted his heart. "*Non*, you are the only American woman for me."

"And the day I believe that, you can sell me the Eiffel Tower, okay?"

He shrugged and pursed his lips again. "I'll give you a good price."

On Ben's last morning in Paris, just as I feared, I could no longer dissuade him from seeing my studio.

"Do you think I came all this way not to see where you've been living for the past three months?"

"It hasn't been three months yet."

"Close enough. Come on, let's go."

Oh Lord. Here we go.

Étienne was at the counter when Ben and I stepped out onto the sidewalk. He waved, and when Ben turned his back, Étienne blew me a kiss. I blew him one back.

"Quit flirting and let's get a move on," Ben said, rolling his eyes.

Oops. "You weren't supposed to see that."

"I wish I hadn't." But he laughed when he said it, as if he was egging me on. It made me feel a little less nervous about showing him my new work.

Until the metro pulled to a screeching stop at the École Militaire stop.

Emerging from the darkness into the neighborhood I'd grown so accustomed to was like entering my own

personal twilight zone. Everything looked the same—
the market stalls on the rue Cler were in full swing; people crowded the streets buying bread, cheese and fresh
produce; the vendors hollered their specials to pas-
sersby—but it all moved in a strange, warped slow-
motion set to the sound track of my thudding heart,
growing more intense as we turned onto the street that
housed the Delacroix Centre.

Ben studied the map in his guidebook as we walked.
"Wait a minute, this is near the Eiffel Tower, right?"

"Right."

"Why didn't we stop by yesterday when we were over
here? I asked you when we were up at the top and you
said—well, you handed me some lame excuse. What
gives, Mom? Why don't you want me to see your place?"

I stopped, at a loss for words. God, when did the kid
get to be so smart? What was I thinking? He'd always
been smart.

"Oh, Ben, come here." We sat on a low stone wall
about forty yards down from the center. He was an adult
now. Maybe if I leveled with him—

"The work I've done here is a lot different from what
I've done in the past. I don't know. I guess I'm just a little nervous about what you're going to think of it."

Of me?

He scrunched up his nose in a manner that was completely his own. "Get over it."

What?

He stood up.

"What did you say?"

"Get over it. You're an artist. Show me your work."

I blinked once. Twice. My God, he was right.

"Okay." I stood up, too. "That's what I thought you said."

Jean Luc's studio was shut up tight, but I noticed Guerrier's cat dish had food in it.

My body tensed.

He'd been there. Not long ago, judging by the amount of food in the bowl.

My hand shook a little as I inserted the key and I wasn't sure if it was because of narrowly missing Jean Luc or because on the walk it dawned on me that I hadn't tried to explain just *how different* my work was from what Ben was used to seeing. I took a steadying breath and reminded myself that he'd been away at school since I started painting again and hadn't seen the flowers. He really had no basis of comparison.

Still, some of the work was pretty bawdy.

I pushed open the door and stepped inside, first giving the place a once-over to make sure I hadn't forgotten to put away anything crucial—like an errant condom packet.

My God, it felt as if we'd switched roles. He was the adult and I was the kid trying to fool him into believing I'd behaved impeccably while I was on my own.

He was already inside looking at the canvases. I held my breath waiting for his critique.

He was silent for about five minutes, looking, slowly walking around the room from canvas to canvas.

While he looked, I busied myself at the table dead-heading the freesias and sweeping up the blossoms that had fallen in my absence.

I should have stopped at the flower market on the rue Cler and bought new flowers—

"This is *your* work?" Ben stared at me wide-eyed.

Oh, no, here it came. I steeled myself, but that didn't extinguish the slow burn that rose from my belly upward.

"God, Mom. Why are you all red? These are cool."

I shrugged and crushed a dead freesia blossom between my fingers.

"You really painted these?"

I nodded and felt myself start to breathe again.

He liked them. My son liked the hookers and cross-dressers and transsexuals of Pigalle. God, after what happened with his father I would *never* tell him most of the *women* I'd painted were actually men. When I went back up there with Jean Luc—he insisted I shouldn't go alone—I was amazed at how some of the most beautiful of the bunch were actually men or beings caught in limbo between the sexes, thanks to hormones and plastic surgery. It was amazing. Some of the *men* actually make me feel unfeminine.

"Wow." Shaking his head, Ben started another circle around the room "You're really talented. No wonder they brought you to Paris."

"Choose the one you like and you can take it with you."

It was a test to see if he actually wanted one. I mean, I couldn't imagine him explaining to his dorm mates his mother was the artist.

"Really?"

But when he started picking up canvases and comparing them, eliminating some and narrowing down others, I realized he was serious. I also realized if I was ever going to move ahead on this solo journey, I did need, in the famous words of my son, to get over it.

I needed to hold my head up proud.

This is my work.

I experienced one last pang of weirdness when I wondered if I should tell Ben exactly what he was looking at…

But what was he looking at? What did *he* see?

A sensual woman or a man in drag?

It wasn't as if he were going to take the person home and unwrap him later and get the surprise of his life.

The interpretation of art should be left to the beholder.

The melodic sound of Matilde's laughter snapped me out of philosophizing. My attention snapped to the door and I saw her and Jean Luc outside of his studio.

For a moment, he stood transfixed, looking at me. I couldn't tell if it was a guilty look or one meant to say, *This is what you get.*

My gaze slid to Matilde; she looked at me as if see-ing a ghost and all of a sudden I felt as if she'd slid her milky-white hands around my neck and started squeez-ing the life out of me.

I couldn't breathe as I glanced back at the bizarre Pigalle freak show lining my wall, and back at her.

Suddenly it was crystal clear why Jean Luc had been so evasive when it came to Matilde. Oh God, it all added up: Pigalle, the beautiful elusive Matilde, Jean Luc's tight-lipped silence… Oh God.

Was Matilde a transsexual?

Was Jean Luc… I couldn't even say it.

The night I saw her modeling for him in his studio, she wore a G-string. On one of our trips to Pigalle, when I asked how transsexuals could parade in skimpy-next-to-nothings without ruining the "illusion of fem-ininity," Jean Luc told me they "hid their candy."

They "tucked it away" so seamlessly that they could get away with short-shorts and G-strings.

I grabbed the back of the chair to steady myself. Why didn't it dawn on me sooner? How else would he have known all the sordid details?

"*Who* is the blonde?" Ben asked. "She's hot."

I almost fell over myself on my way to the door.

"She's nobody." Jean Luc had called her *nobody*, too, that very first day.

With a quick flick of my wrist, I slammed the door.

* * *

There was a note on my door when I got back from taking Ben to the airport.

Annabelle,
    I must see you. It is most urgent. Please.
    JLLG

He wanted to see me. Well, I didn't want to see him. Noooo. Fool me once, shame on me. Fool me twice—

No! He knew what I'd gone through with Blake, yet he'd intentionally led me on a chase. He knew it was my most vulnerable, raw, exposed nerve. My supposedly heterosexual husband left me for a man. Here Jean Luc was a switch-hitter who played on my vulnerability. I didn't care if he liked women *some of the time*.

Some of the time didn't get it. No. I was a full-time, one-man–one-woman show. How dare he do this to me.

I threw open the door and strode across the court-yard ready to tell him the *most urgent* things that were on my mind.

I didn't even knock. I threw open the door.

"How in the hell could you—"

Matilde stood in the middle of the floor.

Sans thong.

Totally nude. Most definitely, one-hundred-percent female. Unless she'd had some sort of miracle surgery that transformed her—

Jean Luc looked up from the big block of marble he'd been chipping away at with a hammer and chisel.

All I could manage was, "Oh!"

Matilde didn't even bother to cover herself. She looked startlingly thin and I noticed tiny bruises marring the ivory skin of her arms.

Another act for my Pigalle freak show?

Nah, I'd had my fill.

Jean Luc stood, looking surprised to see me, but not angry.

"Annabelle?"

I turned and walked out, trying to sort out if Matilde being a woman was a good thing or not. It was definitely better than *her* being a *him*. But then there was the small matter of her being there at all since the extent of what Jean Luc would tell me about her was that her work for him was finished.

I guess the hiring freeze had melted.

I'd just closed the door when it opened again. Jean Luc rushed in, his eyes looking wild.

"Please talk to me," he implored. "Where have you been? I have been worried sick about you."

Excuse me? Where have I been?

"I have nothing to say to you."

I went into the bedroom and shut the door.

Jean Luc pounded on it. "I am not leaving until we talk about this."

Realizing he probably meant what he said, I opened the door. "Okay, start talking." I glanced at my watch. "You have exactly two minutes."

He tried to take my hand. "Let's sit down or go get some coffee or a glass of wine—"

"You now have one minute and forty-five seconds."

He dropped my hand and turned his back to me, throwing his hands in the air and balling them into fists as if it helped him contain his frustration.

"How could you lie to me?" I said, unable to hold it in any longer. The tears I'd held back since the morning he walked out of my studio more than a week ago flowed in torrents.

"I didn't—I mean, I know how it must look."

That was the *worst* thing he could have said.

"Stop it!" I screamed. "You told me she was gone and she's in your studio. You disappear for days, handing me a lame excuse about final exams and all the while you were with her—"

"Anna, listen to me. That's not the case—"

"I don't want your excuses."

I put my hands over my ears. He started to say something about reasons and explanations, but I cut him off.

"The only thing I'm willing to listen to is if you tell me who this woman is and what she means to you. And I want her in here so she can hear what you tell me."

He shrugged. "She doesn't speak English and you're not fluent in French so I don't know what that will solve. Anna, if you will sit down, I will tell you everything."

He looked so earnest that I sat and stared at his sad, handsome face as he told me Matilde was a prostitute and heroin addict.

"Didn't you see the track marks on her arms? How thin she'd gotten?"

He looked at me but I didn't say anything.

So he started from the beginning. He met her when she modeled for his class at Beaux-Arts.

"I admit that she is incredibly beautiful and in the beginning I was interested in her. Until I learned of her way of life. I promise you…" He touched my arm, but I pulled away. "I swear upon my father's good name that I have never made love with her."

He paused and looked at me, his eyes beseeching me to believe him. They may not have made love—was that what we did?—but I wanted to ask him if they'd had *sex*. Down-and-dirty-what's-love-got-to-do-with-it sex. It's amazing how men can justify that there's a difference.

"It's a good thing we did not." He paused for a minute, swallowing against the emotion mounting in his voice. "Anna, she has AIDS."

Oh God.

"All I wanted to do was help her get off the street and get clean. That's why I gave her all the work I could afford, but it wasn't enough to support her *habits*. She would not quit."

I stared at him, stunned speechless. He buried his face in his hands for a moment, then raked his hands through his hair.

"That night you and I met in the Pigalle café, that night you followed me when I walked Matilde home. I knew she had been shooting up again. She missed a couple of our sessions and I finally leveled the ultimatum. Either she quit the drugs or she was no longer welcome in my studio. That night she did not know she had been infected."

His angry words and the sadness in his eyes crushed me. He looked down, studied his hands. "The day we drove down to Cannes—"

My blood ran cold. I knew what he was going to say before he said it. "She was the business you had to take care of?"

He nodded but still wouldn't look at me. I hated myself for it, but pangs of jealousy coursed through me. I knew I should feel bad for this woman who'd been handed a death sentence, but just looking at him I knew he had feelings for Matilde. He and Matilde *would* have been lovers had she chosen him over sex for drugs and money.

Even if he didn't make love to Matilde, it was evident he loved her.

Of course he did.

She was beautiful. And young. I was just a substitute to pass the time with. I bristled at the irony. Just as I could not compete with a man for Blake's affections, I couldn't—*wouldn't* compete with the young, gorgeous, tragic Matilde for Jean Luc. The playing field was not level, and my heart was still too bruised and tender to have it ripped out and torn apart again.

"You love her."

He shook his head, still not looking me in the eyes.

Despite how he denied it, the woman had a hold on him.

"Jean Luc, it doesn't matter. I am going back to Florida in two weeks. You can love her and take care of her. You can do all the things you feel you need to do. Just do it."

"No, Anna, I do not want you to go."

I opened my mouth to speak, but all that came out was a perplexed grunt. A most unladylike, undignified sound, but I was so flummoxed by the whole turn of events I couldn't muster anything else.

"Please tell me you will consider staying in Paris after your residency."

"Doing what? Modeling for you? I can be your lover while Matilde is your love?"

I choked on the words as the tears started flowing again.

"You could stay and paint and write a book about this Camille Deveau who interests you so. You could live with me."

I shook my head, hating him for even mentioning it. Staying in Paris was not an option for me. With the stipend set to end with the residency, what would I do to support myself? I wouldn't live with Jean Luc. Even the thought made me feel too vulnerable.

Once upon a time, I put my life in Blake's hands. What did that get me? Nothing but eighteen years of lies with a chaser of heartache. From now on, I was a one-woman show.

I got up and walked to the door, opened it. "You'll have to go now."

He sat there for a moment, his elbows braced on his knees, contemplating his hands. Then he stood and walked toward me.

"Jean Luc?"

"Yes?"

"Why did you go all the way to Cannes for her?"

He looked me in the eyes. "Earlier that week, Matilde took an overdose. She had learned of her condition and she wanted to…to end it.

"The hospital would not release her unless she was released into the care of someone. She called me because she had no one else."

Of course you went running right down there, didn't you?

I felt myself begin to back away emotionally. If I got caught in the middle of that messed-up relationship, I had no one else but myself to blame. But I still had to know—

"So what happened? You went out that night in Cannes and left me at the house in the tub. What did you do with Matilde?"

He rubbed his hand over his eyes before he looked at me. "I got her from the hospital. She seemed well enough. She wanted to come back to the villa with me—"

"Had you taken her there before?"

"No."

"Then how did she know about it?"

"She grew up in Antibes, which is twenty minutes from Cannes. When I first met her and learned of her association with the area, I told her my family spent time in Cannes. She knew of the Villa Angeline right away. She'd always wanted me to take her there."

"You didn't invite her to join us?" I knew it was a mean thing to say, but I couldn't help it.

He arched a brow and gave me a what-do-you-think shrug. "I told her she could not come to the villa because you were there. She ran away from me. I spent most of the time I was gone driving around looking for her—"

A chill passed over me. "She was there, wasn't she? She was the one inside the house." My hand flew to my mouth.

He bowed his head. "Yes, it was she. She told me as much." He searched my eyes. "She would never hurt you. She's not like that."

He touched my arm but I pulled away. I'd heard as much as I wanted to know. Just knowing she was there, looking at me as I lay in the tub, made every nerve in my body stand at red alert. I gestured at the door, hoping he would just go, because I was slowly coming undone.

"You must know she is only back for a short while. Just until she finishes this job for me."

"Until next time. Because there's always going to be a next time. You realize that, don't you?"

He squinted at me as if he didn't understand what I meant. But I didn't feel like explaining.

"May I see you tonight?" he said.

I shook my head, realizing he really didn't get it.

"No, Jean Luc, I can't see you anymore. I have to get ready for the end-of-residency exhibit. You might say, I have to prepare for my own final exam."

After five days without as much as a glimpse of Jean Luc, I realized he was honoring my request for him to leave me alone.

It was the best for all parties involved. Matilde needed him, he was devoted to her, and I had grown too fond of him for my own good.

I should have known I was not the kind of woman who could casually sleep with someone and write it off as a European fling. I envied women who could detach themselves that way. I wasn't cut from that cloth. I would have been lying if I said I didn't wonder where they'd gone. His studio was locked up tight. I didn't know if they'd gone elsewhere and started work on another project or—

It didn't matter.

I had the end-of-residency show to worry about. The way it worked was each resident chose five pieces to display in his or her studio. One week before the residency officially ended was the "studio walk." Jauvert, a center board member, an official from the City of Paris and one from the French Ministry of Foreign Affairs would walk into each studio and choose the one piece they deemed the best of the work displayed. That piece would be on exhibit in the gallery for the last week of the residency term.

The night before we bid each other *adieu* they would announce the winner of the one-hundred-thousand-dollar purchase prize.

I was proud of the work I'd produced.

Viewing it as a whole, I felt like I was ready to show what I'd accomplished. *Let's see if I lived up to Jauvert's expectation that I would be the most improved.*

Frankly, I didn't care what he thought. I'd taken Ben's advice and *gotten over it.*

I chose four works from the Pigalle series, and just to throw Jauvert a curveball, I included *The Bed.*

As I set up for the studio walk, I almost chickened out of including it among the five. Out of respect to Jean Luc—it was his image captured in a most intimate moment.

If he'd been around, I would have asked his permission, but he wasn't. I could only go on gut instinct. Embarrassment didn't keep him from hanging the painting front and center on the living-room wall.

I sensed he would probably consider it an honor if I included it in the show.

I certainly hoped so, because the jury ended up choosing it as my entry in the end-of-residency show.

CHAPTER 17

Jean Luc returned the day before they announced the winner of the purchase prize. Since he'd been gone, I felt I owed it to him to tell him *The Bed* was selected for the show.

I stopped to pet Guerrier as I walked across the courtyard to talk to Jean Luc.

"I am going to miss you when I go back to the States," I said as I stroked the cat.

Jean Luc must have heard me talking to Guerrier because he came to the door holding his hammer and chisel, his jeans and gray shirt covered in a fine dust, before I even had a chance to knock.

"Is Matilde inside?" I didn't know why I asked. I didn't care if she was. Well, not much, anyway.

He shook his head. His hair looked glossy and almost black in the shadow of the doorway. "She is gone."

"Where did she go?" Guerrier rolled over on his side so I could scratch his belly.

"She has gone to London to a residential treatment center that specializes in treating people with AIDS."

I wondered how long it would take her to come

bounding back into his life. I stood up and brushed the cat hair from my hands. "Jean Luc, she obviously loves you very much."

He shrugged. "I care for her very deeply, too. Just not in the way you assume. That is why I sent her to London. I hoped it would make you see that you are the person I care about."

That old familiar longing tugged at the pit of my stomach and I remembered with startling clarity the last time we made love. I tried to blink away the image.

"I'm not sure how you'll feel about me after you hear what I have to say."

He crossed his arms. "Why don't you come inside."

The sun beat down and it was turning out to be one of the warmest days we'd had since I'd arrived. Cooler than in Florida, but still warm enough to entice me to step inside his studio.

He went to the refrigerator and pulled out a bottle of Perrier and a lime.

He didn't ask me if I wanted some, just poured two glasses.

"So what is it you fear will change my opinion of you?"

He set a glass in front of me. "*The Bed*, er, my painting, *The Bed*, it's in the end-of-residency show. Jauvert and his band of merry men chose it as my entry."

He nodded. "Very good. Congratulations. What was your concern?"

I picked up the glass and sipped. "That you might not want it in the show."

He smiled. "Not to worry. I am honored."

He put the water and lime back in the refrigerator, then picked up a box off his work bench. It was about the size of a shirt box and was tied with a red ribbon.

"This is for you."

A wave of apprehension swept through me. "Jean Luc, no. I can't."

"After Matilde left, I went back to Cannes. You see, there was another reason I brought you down there with me that day. There is an old woman in Cannes— a distant cousin of Camille Deveau's. Her last living relative. She holds some of her possessions. I asked some of my contacts at the École des Beaux-Arts and learned of her. I had to—how you say—jump through hoops, but I met her and obtained permission to copy Camille Deveau's remaining letters and her diaries. *Voilà*, for you, *madame*. What's more, she said she might be interested in working with someone to publish them. She has long thought that Camille would like the truth about her relationship with Georges Fonteneau to be known, that somehow it would validate their relationship. She said she did not know how to go about it, but would assist someone interested in researching and writing the book. You wouldn't know of anyone, would you?"

He held out the box and this time I accepted it, bewildered and bemused that he would go to so much trouble to do this for me. All I managed to stammer was, "Thank you."

"Anna, perhaps Camille has chosen you to tell her story and win her the recognition she is due?" Jean Luc said. "Can you really walk away from that?"

The correspondence filled in the missing pieces of Camille Deveau's story. She and Georges Fonteneau were lovers deeply, passionately in love. They never married because he was not able to obtain a divorce from his wife. When it all became too painful, she moved to Cannes to free herself from the one love she could never have.

Was she right in running away?

What would have happened if she'd stayed?

Even she pondered these questions, admittedly after it was too late.

The last page in the collection didn't have anything to do with Camille Deveau. It was from Jean Luc.

May I please have the honor of escorting you to the farewell reception?

JLLG

In a perfect world, this is how I envisioned the end-of-residency award ceremony unfolding:

I would don a brand-new outfit purchased just for the

occasion, a sexy red number that hugged me in all the right places, and new strappy sandals that looked very French, of course. I'd leave my hair down and let it curl exactly how it wanted to, and at precisely five minutes until eight o'clock, Jean Luc would knock on my door. He would take my hand and we would start toward the Delacroix Gallery.

At this point in my growth I would no longer care about being the first to arrive. I'd have transcended the stigma of caring what the others thought of me.

Jean Luc would open the heavy wooden gallery door for me and the first thing I would see when I entered was *The Bed* hanging front and center on the gallery wall. Then I'd vaguely register the Parisian Barbies who'd be talking to Jacques Jauvert. All three heads would swivel in our direction.

Jacques Jauvert would say, "*Bonsoir*, Madame Essex and Monsieur Le Garric."

We would return the greeting.

The Parisian Barbies would *bonsoir* in unison, and stand there perfectly coiffed and made up, holding their wineglasses by the stem, dainty pinkies extended, the same as they had that first night. I would wonder if Jauvert simply took them out of their boxes and set them on the floor for such occasions.

Jauvert would probably make some crack about my punctuality, but I would be secure enough to realize it wasn't personal, just his attempt to make conversation.

I would seize this opportunity to introduce myself to

the attending members of the press and dignitaries from the City of Paris and the French Ministry of Foreign Affairs. After three months, I would be confident enough in the French I'd learned that I could carry on a basic conversation. Of course, they would be quite impressed at my willingness to communicate with them in their own language, but since they all spoke English fluently they'd help me out when I'd backed myself into a language corner.

Jean Luc and I would barely have enough time to wander around the gallery and look at the twelve pieces of artwork, each one accomplished in its own right, before the others would arrive; some looking even more anxious than they did that first evening three months ago.

But I would be calm and cool, not from overconfidence but because I was happy with my experience in Paris and the resulting work I'd produced. After all, wasn't that the real prize?

Mr. Argentina would nod to me, but rather than indulge the petty part of myself and wonder if he had an unfair edge for the hundred thousand since he and Jauvert were obviously involved, instead, I would nod back. I would probably even smile.

I might purposely make eye contact with Lesya Sokolov, the mixed-media artist from Romania. The faintest hint of a smile would tip the corners of her mouth, a sincere smile of solidarity. Even though we hadn't carried on a single conversation while at the

NANCY ROBARDS THOMPSON   *293*

center, I'd realize it was okay. I'd intuitively under-stand that we'd both found what we'd been seeking in Paris.

Although I'd still be the oldest person in the bunch, with the exception of the effeminate European painter, and the men who'd stood in a group on that first night would still huddle in an impenetrable clique, I would understand that was okay; that to the untrained eye, even though we all appeared very much the same as we did that first day, we were all leaving different people; that sometimes you have to look deeper to discover what's really there.

Even though I wouldn't have given much thought to the evening's announcement of the winner, my stomach would probably tighten in anticipation when Jacques Jauvert tapped his Montblanc pen on his wine-glass and everyone gathered around the podium.

I would listen politely as he said, "Much of what this program encourages is the artist's personal self-discovery and growth. The jury was not only looking to purchase a great piece of artwork for the collection at the Museum of American Exchange, but also for evidence of how the artist had incorporated him- or herself into the body of work produced at the Delacroix Centre. For we believe self-discovery cannot be taught. It is up to the artist to seek what stimulates and appropriately apply it to his or her work."

Then he would commend each and every one of us

for our talent and dedication, and say, "There was one artist whose work unanimously captured the fancy of the selection committee...."

Even though I would be perfectly fine no matter who was named the winner, my mouth might go dry in the split seconds before Jauvert announced, "The winner of the Delacroix purchase prize award is, *The Bed* by Annabelle Essex."

My name would sound as if it had been called through an echo chamber. Every gaze in the room would turn to me and the gallery would reverberate with applause. Jauvert would motion for me to join him up front and the edges of my peripheral vision would turn white and wavy, enhanced by the strobe of camera flash exploding around me.

I would feel Jean Luc's steady hand touch my elbow. Then in slow motion, he would bend down and kiss me and we would share a private smile that would seem to last a lifetime, but all this would happen in the span of a few seconds. Jean Luc would take my wineglass, and somehow my feet would propel me forward toward Jacques Jauvert and the podium where he would quickly air kiss both of my cheeks; so would the group of dignitaries from the City of Paris and the French Ministry of Foreign Affairs.

All the while I would look at Jean Luc, who would smile his George Clooney smile, with one brow arched in a way that lit a flame deep inside me.

When quiet returned, Jauvert would continue, "In the fifteen years I've headed the exchange program, we've never granted a residency based on one piece of work."

I might start to worry, *Oh, no. Not that again*, but I would catch myself before I did. The old me would have done that. Now, it wouldn't bother me the way it did that first night.

Jacques Jauvert would say something about anticipating much growth from me and how I didn't disappoint him and the other members of the jury.

Then, just when I thought the evening couldn't get any better, Jauvert would present me with an oversize check for one hundred thousand dollars.

I would graciously accept it and think, *I knew I liked him from the beginning, I just had to grow into it.*

Then after all the excitement faded and Jean Luc and I found ourselves alone, I wouldn't waste time worrying about all the what-ifs and should've's and could've's that can make a person crazy.

He would pull me into his arms and say, "Anna, I love you. Please stay and walk beside me in this world."

I would say, "Of course I will, because I love you, too."

We would know that all that mattered was what was happening at that moment, that even though I had gone "Faraway" to find myself I'd come full circle in my journey.

Yes, in a perfect world, what was supposed to be my

last evening in Paris would become the first day of the rest of my life with a lover I trusted and a career I loved.

Sometimes, when you want things badly enough all the stars line up, and for one perfect night you get that perfect world....

Three friends,
two exes
and a plan
to get payback.

The Payback Club
by Rexanne Becnel
USA TODAY BESTSELLING AUTHOR

HARLEQUIN®

Next™

Artist-in-Residence Fellowship–
Call for applications

She always dreamed of studying art in Paris,
but as a wife and mother she has had
other things to do. Finally, Anna is taking
a chance on her own.

What Happens in Paris

(STAYS IN PARIS?)

Nancy Robards Thompson

Mothers, sisters and other passengers

Novelist Maggie Dufrane's mama is the Mississippi queen of drama. When her sister Jean drops a shocker on the family, Mama thinks it's the best gossip she's heard all year. But it's up to reliable Maggie-the-family-chauffeur to fix things...again.

Driving Me Crazy

PEGGY WEBB

HN27TTALL

Available January 2006
TheNextNovel.com

A woman determined to walk her own path

Joining a gym was the last thing Janine ever expected to do. But with each step on that treadmill, a new world of possibilities was opening up!

TREADING LIGHTLY
ELISE LANIER

eHARLEQUIN.com

The Ultimate Destination for Women's Fiction

The eHarlequin.com online community is *the* place to share opinions, thoughts and feelings!

- Joining the community is easy, fun and **FREE!**

- Connect with **other romance fans** on our message boards.

- Meet your **favorite authors** without leaving home!

- **Share opinions** on books, movies, celebrities…and *more!*

Here's what our members say:

"I love the friendly and helpful atmosphere filled with support and humor."
—Texanna (eHarlequin.com member)

"Is this the place for me, or what? There is nothing I love more than 'talking' books, especially with fellow readers who are reading the same ones I am."
—Jo Ann (eHarlequin.com member)

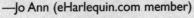

**Join today by visiting
www.eHarlequin.com!**

What happens when new friends get together and dig into the past?

Ex's and Oh's
Sandra Steffen

A story about secrets, surprises
and relationships.

Sometimes the craziness of living
the perfect suburban life is enough
to make a woman wonder…

Who makes up these rules, Anyway?

BY
STEVI MITTMAN

Since when did life ever tell you where you were going?

Sometimes you just have to dip your oar into the water and start to paddle.

THE
SUNSHINE
COAST
NEWS

KATE AUSTIN